*"The most important consideration for any samurai
is how to behave at the moment of death."*

Samurai Code of Taira Shigesuke

Shadow of the NINJA

ANDREW MATTHEWS

USBORNE

Characters

SAMURAI
Jimmu Shimomura
Ryu Yasuda

CHOJU CLAN, MITSUKAGE CASTLE
Lord Ankan, Jimmu's master
Lady Takeko, Lord Ankan's daughter

ODA CLAN, NAGASHINO CASTLE
Lord Nobunaga, ally of Choju Clan

TAKEDA CLAN
Lord Shingen, deceased, enemy of Choju Clan
Katsuyori, son of Lord Shingen

HIKI CLAN, TOKORO CASTLE
Lord Yoshinori, deceased leader, ally of Lord Ankan
Lord Sabura, Yoshinori's son, ally of Takeda Clan
Aki, maid to Lady Takeko
Sora, maid to Lady Takeko

NINJAS
Goro, master ninja
Ichiro, cousin of Yasada Ryu
Yuki, wife of Ichiro
Ren

For Ben, Gemma and Matilda
with love

Editorial consultant: Tony Bradman

First published in the UK in 2010 by Usborne Publishing Ltd., Usborne House, 83-85 Saffron Hill, London EC1N 8RT, England. www.usborne.com
Copyright © Andrew Matthews, 2010

The right of Andrew Matthews to be identified as the author of this work has been asserted by him in accordance with the Copyright, Designs and Patents Act, 1988.

Cover illustration by Neil Francis.

The name Usborne and the devices ♕ 🎈 are Trade Marks of Usborne Publishing Ltd.

A CIP catalogue record for this book is available from the British Library.

JFMA JJASOND/10 00542/1 ISBN 9781409506201

Printed in Reading, Berkshire, UK.

Chapter 1

All the lamps had been lit in the prayer hall of the monastery, and the gilded statue of Buddha gleamed on its plinth. Near the foot of the statue, an old monk and a young man sat facing each other, talking quietly, while the night wind sighed through the branches of the forest that stood outside the monastery walls.

The monk's name was Naoki. He had once had another name and another life. In his younger days he had been a samurai with a fearsome reputation, but at the height of his fame he had given up everything to follow the way of Buddha. A year ago the young man, Jimmu, had arrived at Okamori, and begged Naoki to tutor him, so that he could improve his fighting skills. Naoki had agreed, on condition that Jimmu also studied prayer and meditation. Over time, their mutual respect had deepened into affection, and Naoki had come to regard Jimmu as an honorary grandson.

They made a contrasting pair. Naoki was bald. His muscular physique had shrunk with age, and his face was deeply lined. Jimmu was tall and slim. He wore his hair tied back in a style that emphasized his high cheekbones, and the intense expression in his eyes.

Naoki had summoned Jimmu to him and now, with great reluctance, he came to the point of their conversation. "We've come to the end of what I can teach you, Jimmu," he said. "You're a better samurai than I was at your age. The question is, do you feel ready to return to Lord Choju Ankan's service?"

Jimmu nodded. "Meditation has helped me to prepare myself," he said. "I was brought up to believe that Lord Ankan caused my father's death. I went to Mitsukage Castle seeking revenge. When I first learned that what I believed was a lie, it came as a great shock. Now I've recovered, I no longer blame myself for my mistake."

"And Lady Choju Takeko?" Naoki enquired.

"I esteem her as Lord Ankan's daughter," said Jimmu.

Naoki clicked his tongue, and rolled his eyes. "Speak honestly!" he scolded. "You admitted to me that your feelings for her went far beyond esteem – as did her feelings for you."

Jimmu thought carefully before replying. "I've spent the last two years on a warrior pilgrimage," he said. "For the first year, I travelled. In Nagasaki, I met traders from countries far across the ocean. I learned more about the world, and what I learned changed me. I think perhaps Lady Takeko has changed too."

"Do you *think* she has changed, or do you fear that she has?" said Naoki.

Jimmu looked down at his hands. "My personal feelings aren't important," he said. "A samurai's first duty is to obey his master. I won't let anything distract me from that."

Naoki nodded. "That was the answer I was hoping for," he said. "If you keep your duty firmly in mind, your uncertainties will disappear. Go back to Mitsukage Castle with my blessing. As the river finds the sea, may you find peace and understanding."

Jimmu stood up, bowed low, and left the prayer hall.

*

The journey took several days. Jimmu travelled mostly on foot, though occasionally a friendly farmer offered him a ride on an ox cart. At last, he came in sight of Mitsukage Castle, and paused to gaze at it.

The morning light slanted shadows across the castle's tiled roofs with their curved eaves. Where the sunshine touched them, the walls shone white.

Like a swan – or a ghost, Jimmu thought.

Memories that he had been holding back flooded through his mind. He reached inside his jerkin, and closed his fingers over the little red jade horse that he wore on a leather cord fastened around his neck. Takeko had given it to him as a memento. Jimmu recalled the day she bought it at a winter fair in the village of Sakura.

We were like children playing a game of make-believe, he told himself. I should have been stronger, and kept away from her.

The jade horse mocked him. If he really believed that his relationship with Takeko was wrong, why had he kept it?

Jimmu walked on. With every step he took, the castle grew more familiar, and at the same time more strange.

He knew its layout and its routines; it was the closest thing to a home that he had ever known. Yet he had seen more impressive fortresses in the course of his pilgrimage. Mitsukage was smaller than he remembered. During his absence, Jimmu had often dreamed about the place; the reality was slightly disappointing.

When Jimmu knocked at the main gate, the shutter of a spyhole was pulled back, and a familiar scarred face peered out.

"Hello, Kambei," said Jimmu.

The old guard's mouth spread wide in a grin that showed more gaps than teeth. "Jimmu!" he gurgled.

Kambei opened the gate. Jimmu passed through, and Kambei clapped him on the back. "Look at you, Jimmu!" he cried. "You've filled out. You're more like a man than a boy. What did you get up to while you were away? Did you go to Kyoto and sample the city's delights? Is it true that the geisha girls there are the most beautiful in all Japan?"

"Gatekeeper Kambei!" shrilled a voice. "Why have you left your post?"

Jimmu turned, and saw a squat figure approaching across the courtyard. It was Captain Hankei, who had been promoted from sergeant shortly before Jimmu left Mitsukage. As always, the captain held himself stiffly, in an attempt to appear taller than he actually was.

Kambei stood to attention. "It's Jimmu, sir!" he explained.

"That's no excuse for negligence!" said the captain. "Resume your duty!"

Kambei saluted, tipping Jimmu a wink as he did so.

Captain Hankei glanced critically at Jimmu. "Welcome, Jimmu!" he said. "Lord Ankan will be pleased to see you – but not while you're dressed like that. You look like a monk."

"I've been living in a monastery," explained Jimmu.

Captain Hankei pursed his lips. "I suggest you visit the bathhouse," he said. "A servant will fetch you some clean clothes. I'll inform Lord Ankan of your arrival, and ask if he wishes to receive you."

"Is His Lordship well?" asked Jimmu.

"He is."

"And Lady Takeko?" said Jimmu.

Captain Hankei's upper lip quivered. "My Lady is in good health," he said.

"Will she be with Lord Ankan in his private chamber?" asked Jimmu.

This enquiry had a startling effect on Captain Hankei. Colour rose to his face, and his eyes bulged. "What business is it of yours?" he spluttered. "Why are you asking so many questions? Have you been listening to rumours? Are you accusing me of neglecting my duty as captain of His Lordship's guards?"

Jimmu was mystified by the captain's outburst. "I'm not accusing anyone of anything," he said.

"Mind you don't!" the captain advised. "And now, if you'll excuse me, I have orders to carry out."

Captain Hankei twirled smartly on his left heel, and marched off.

"What's the matter with him?" Jimmu wondered aloud.

"He's been flapping about like a goose for days," remarked Kambei. "If you ask me, his piles are playing up." He put his head to one side, and spat to ward off bad luck. "Hey, Jimmu! When Lord Ankan has finished with you, come and have a chat. I want to hear all about those Kyoto girls!"

Chapter 2

*L*ord Ankan's private apartment was simply furnished. A low table had been set against one wall, and Lord Ankan's battle armour was displayed on a stand at the far end of the room. His Lordship, dressed in a grey cotton kimono, was seated cross-legged on a rush mat.

Jimmu was dismayed by the change in his master. Lord Ankan's hair, once black, was now steely grey, and his grizzled beard had turned white. There were dark pouches beneath his eyes. Only his voice remained the same, clear and precise. "Welcome, Jimmu," he said. "I have often thought of you over the past two years."

Jimmu bowed low. "I am honoured, My Lord."

Lord Ankan gestured. "Sit down, Jimmu. I have many things to discuss with you."

Jimmu sat, and waited for His Lordship to continue.

"Before I begin, I want your word that you will not reveal what I tell you to anyone else in the castle," said Lord Ankan.

"You have my word, My Lord."

"I intend to be frank with you, Jimmu, and I require you to be frank in return," said Lord Ankan. "Do you agree?"

"Just as you wish, My Lord," Jimmu said.

Lord Ankan nodded. "Good. Let me begin by informing you that I'm aware of the close bond you formed with Lady Takeko before you left Mitsukage."

"My Lord!" protested Jimmu. "Lady Takeko and I did nothing that—"

Lord Ankan raised a hand, and Jimmu fell silent.

"I am not blaming you, Jimmu, and I am not angry," said His Lordship. "I only mention your bond with Takeko in order to protect you."

Jimmu did not follow. "Protect me from what, My Lord?"

"From yourself," said Lord Ankan. "Do you know about the change that has taken place in our rival clan, the Takeda?"

"I heard that your old enemy, Takeda Shingen had died, and that the leadership of the clan passed to his son, Katsuyori," Jimmu said.

Anger glowed in Lord Ankan's eyes. "Takeda Katsuyori grew up in his father's shadow," he declared. "His ambition is to build a reputation even greater than Shingen's. He has the old man's courage, but lacks his patience. The Takeda have laid siege to Nagashino Castle in Mikawa Province. Our friend Lord Oda Nobunaga has called on all his allies, including me, to send him troops. He plans to smash the Takeda once and for all."

"Forgive me, My Lord," said Jimmu, "but I don't understand what any of this has to do with me and Lady Takeko."

"You will understand soon enough," Lord Ankan promised. "A few months after you left, my friend Lord Hiki Yoshinori passed away. His son Sabura became Lord of the Hiki Clan. Lord Sabura came to see me. He told me that his father's dying wish had been for a marriage alliance between our clans, and he requested my permission to court Takeko. I saw no reason to refuse him. Five days ago, he invited Takeko to his castle at Tokoro, to celebrate the Flower Festival," Lord Ankan went on. "He sent a guard of honour to escort her. Once she arrived at the castle, he made her his prisoner."

"But why, My Lord?" Jimmu blurted in astonishment.

"Like Lord Katsuyori, Lord Sabura is young and ambitious," said Lord Ankan. "He has severed his father's alliance with Lord Nobunaga, and sided with the Takeda. If I send troops to support Lord Nobunaga, as he has requested, Lord Sabura threatens to have Takeko put to death."

Jimmu was outraged. "My Lord, attack Tokoro Castle and rescue Lady Takeko!" he urged.

Lord Ankan smiled bitterly. "I wish it were that simple, Jimmu," he said. "If I besiege Tokoro, Lord Nobunaga will be obliged to reinforce me, and that will weaken his forces at a critical time. For that reason, he has forbidden me to take any action against Hiki Sabura."

Jimmu spoke without thinking. "Then you have no choice but to disobey Lord Nobunaga, My Lord!"

"I cannot disobey him," said Lord Ankan. "It

would mean breaking my allegiance. I would be dishonoured as a traitor."

"But Lady Takeko will die!" Jimmu cried.

"I am fully aware of that," said Lord Ankan. "However, I cannot bring myself to behave dishonourably, even at the cost of my daughter's life."

A part of Jimmu was appalled, but another part of him grudgingly admired Lord Ankan's determination: a true warrior valued his honour above everything. "My Lord," he said, "let me pick a few soldiers, and I'll lead a raiding party to free Lady Takeko. We can disguise ourselves as—"

Once again, Lord Ankan raised his hand. "My conscience is troubled enough," he said. "I will not add your death to it. You can serve me best by staying alive, Jimmu. I took you into my confidence because I feared that if you heard a rumour about Takeko, your feelings for her might provoke you into doing something rash. At the end of the month, I will lead my men to Nagashino. I expect you to be among them."

Jimmu saw that he could not say anything to change

his master's mind. He's like a mountain, he thought. Nothing can sway him.

"I have no more to say to you, Jimmu," said Lord Ankan. "The matter is closed. You may leave me."

Jimmu stumbled out of Lord Ankan's private apartment and along the corridor, barely aware of where he was. How could he prevent Takeko's death without going against Lord Ankan's wishes, and breaking the samurai law of obedience?

I'll go to Lord Nobunaga! he thought. If I plead with him, he might take back the order he gave to Lord Ankan.

Jimmu immediately realized how pathetic the hope was. Oda Nobunaga was a great lord who wanted to be the supreme ruler in Japan. Thousands of soldiers had already died in the struggle to achieve his aim. Why should he care about the life of one young woman?

"Jimmu!"

Jimmu started, turned, and saw Captain Hankei lurking near the door that led out into the courtyard.

The captain beckoned him closer, and spoke in a low voice. "Has His Lordship told you about Lady Takeko?"

"Yes."

"You must be as concerned about him as I am," Captain Hankei murmured. "His fear for his daughter grows stronger every day. He doesn't sleep, and barely eats. If things go on as they are, his anxiety will either kill him or drive him mad. I blame myself for not seeing through Lord Sabura's treachery. If I could do something to make amends to His Lordship, I would, but I'm captain of the guard. I have to set an example to the men under my command, not go running off after glory — and it *would* be glorious to rescue Lady Takeko, and bring her back safe and sound."

Jimmu frowned. "Are you suggesting that I should—"

"I'm suggesting nothing," said Captain Hankei. "I'm just saying that someone ought to do something to ease Lord Ankan's mind before the strain gets too much for him. You know how he feels about his daughter."

Jimmu remembered an evening when he had seen Takeko floating paper lanterns across the pool in the castle garden. Lord Ankan had stood nearby, gazing tenderly at her.

"He cares for her deeply," Jimmu said.

"If I were a younger man, with no responsibilities, I'd take a horse from the stables, ride south-east to Tokoro and—" Captain Hankei broke off with a shrug. "But wishing achieves nothing." He lifted his hand in a salute. "Good day, Jimmu."

As he watched Captain Hankei walk off along the corridor, questions swirled through Jimmu's mind. The captain had seemed to be suggesting that Jimmu should ignore what Lord Ankan had told him.

Jimmu was torn between his duty, and his personal feelings for Takeko.

If I obey His Lordship, and Takeko dies, how will I live with myself? he wondered.

The thought ended Jimmu's confusion. He would go to Tokoro Castle and free Takeko, or die in the attempt.

Lady Choju Takeko was kneeling on the floor of the room reserved for the most honoured guests at Tokoro Castle. In front of her stood a low table, set with bowls of untasted food. She was dressed in a white silk kimono, with a black sash tied around her waist. The strain of imprisonment had taken some of the shine from Takeko's black hair and dark eyes, but she was still beautiful.

Takeko stiffened as the door of the room slid open, and Lord Sabura came in. He was a handsome man, with finely arched nostrils and a neatly trimmed moustache, but there was a hint of cruelty in the set of his mouth. His black silk kimono was embroidered with a pattern of flowers and dragons, worked in threads of gold and scarlet.

Lord Sabura crossed the room, made an elaborate bow, and sat down on the opposite side of the table. He glanced at the bowls of food, and frowned. "You have not eaten, Takeko!" he said. "Is the food not to your liking?"

"Being held here against my will isn't to my liking!" said Takeko.

Lord Sabura ignored the comment. "You will make yourself ill if you refuse to eat. Of course, if you prefer, I could have you forcibly fed."

"What does it matter whether I'm ill or not?"

said Takeko. "You're going to kill me!"

"I am sure it will not come to that," Lord Sabura assured her. "In the end, Lord Ankan will see sense, and agree to my terms."

"You don't know my father!" snapped Takeko.

Lord Sabura gestured with his fan. "I rather think I do," he said. "Lord Ankan is like my late father was – proud, gruff and old-fashioned."

"Is that why you murdered him?" said Takeko.

"My revered father clung to traditional ways, traditional alliances," Lord Sabura replied. "He did not see where the best future lay for the Hiki Clan. He was an obstacle to progress, and it became necessary for me to remove that obstacle." Lord Sabura shrugged. "Let us not speak of the past. I have news that I believe will raise your spirits."

"You've decided to set me free?" said Takeko.

"I hear that a certain young samurai has returned to Mitsukage Castle," Lord Sabura said.

"Jimmu?"

Lord Sabura pretended to have difficulty in remembering. "Was that the name? It may have been..."

"How is he?" asked Takeko. "When did he return to Mitsukage? Has he changed much?"

"If you eat a little, I might tell you what I know," Lord Sabura said. "There again, I might not."

Takeko narrowed her eyes. "You take pleasure in tormenting me, don't you?"

"Oh, yes!" said Lord Sabura. "A great deal of pleasure, my dear." His face and voice hardened. "Now, eat!"

Takeko took up a pair of chopsticks from the table. She knew better than to push Lord Sabura too far: beneath the polite mask that he wore, Hiki Sabura was a monster.

Chapter 3

Jimmu left Mitsukage Castle at sunset, riding a bay mare. Lord Ankan's stable master had selected the horse, after Jimmu told him that he was on a special mission for His Lordship. At the Armoury, the same half-truth had provided Jimmu with a breastplate and helmet, which he stowed in the saddlebags, with a bow and a sheaf of arrows. Finally he had gone to Captain Hankei and asked for money, which the captain had given without asking why Jimmu needed it.

Jimmu was relieved that he had put aside his doubts and uncertainties. He had no idea what he would do when he reached Tokoro Castle, but he was confident that something would occur to him. Staying in Mitsukage Castle would achieve nothing; it was vital for him to take action.

As the sunset darkened into dusk, Jimmu became

increasingly convinced that he was being followed. Once or twice, he turned his head to look behind him, but the deepening shadows made it impossible to be sure. In the end, Jimmu ignored his uneasy feeling.

Why would anyone follow me? he asked himself. Stopping to check will only waste time.

It was a decision he would regret later.

Three or four hours after nightfall, the wind picked up, and it began to rain. Jimmu pressed on for as long as he could, but the rain grew torrential, and when a peal of thunder and a bolt of lightning startled the mare and caused her to rear, he realized that he would have to take shelter somewhere. He searched for a bamboo grove, or a thicket of trees that would offer cover, but he found nothing but flooded ditches, and clumps of thorn bushes. Then, just as Jimmu thought that his luck had failed him, he saw a light. He rode towards it, and came to a track that led to an inn at the side of the road.

The inn was not inviting. Its wooden walls were weather-beaten, and the roof needed rethatching. A ragged flag that fluttered over the porch proclaimed the inn's name as, "The Fortunate Swallows".

Jimmu weighed his options. The inn beds would probably be teeming with fleas and lice, but he could sleep on the floor, and there would be a stable for the mare.

When he reached the inn yard, Jimmu dismounted, and fastened the mare to a hitching post. As Jimmu was untying his saddlebags, a man who bobbed his head in a quick bow approached him. "Shall I take your horse for you, sir?" he asked.

Jimmu's fingers fumbled in a purse he wore at his waist, and he produced a coin, which he held out. "Give her a proper rub down," he instructed the man, "and be gentle with her. Thunder and lightning make her jumpy."

The man took the coin. "Don't you worry, sir," he assured Jimmu. "I know all about horses."

The interior of The Fortunate Swallows was as shabby as the outside. The floor of the main room was covered with rotten matting, and in places rainwater dripped through gaps in the roof. A plump man sat behind a roughly made table, so busy eating rice that he did not look up when Jimmu entered. Four men were gambling at another table. One of the gamblers wore an eyepatch. He stared hard at Jimmu with his remaining eye, but looked away when Jimmu stared back.

A greasy dumpling of a man appeared in the doorway of a back room. He bowed to Jimmu. "Esteemed sir, your presence does us honour!" he gushed. "My name is Nobu, and I am landlord here. Do you need a bed for the night?"

Jimmu nodded.

"How else may I provide for your comfort?" Nobu went on. "A hot meal – a bottle of sake to keep out the cold?"

"Food, but no sake," replied Jimmu.

"Certainly, sir," Nobu said. "Potboy!" he shouted into the back room. "Bring noodles!" He smiled at Jimmu, and spread his hands. "If sir would care to choose a table..."

The potboy turned out to be an elderly man who regarded customers as a nuisance. He sighed wearily as he placed a bowl of noodles in front of Jimmu.

Because his samurai training had taught him to consider food as nothing more than fuel for his body, Jimmu paid little attention to his meal, but he was aware that the gamblers kept glancing slyly at him. They nudged one another, and whispered out of the sides of their mouths.

The man with the eyepatch gestured to Jimmu. "Samurai, why don't you come and share our sake, and try your luck?"

Jimmu's answer was coldly polite. "Thank you," he said, "but I don't drink or gamble."

"Suit yourself," said the man. He muttered something to his companions, and they sniggered.

Jimmu guessed that the gamblers were having a joke at his expense, but decided to ignore it. He had met men like them before, in the taverns of Kyoto: men who drank too freely, and then picked quarrels because they enjoyed the excitement of the fight. Jimmu followed the Samurai Code, and avoided petty squabbles. If real trouble found him, he would deal with it, but he refused to seek it out unnecessarily.

Just then, the door of the inn crashed open, and a samurai lurched into the room as if he had been blown in by a strong gust of wind. He was a middle-aged man of medium height, with a muscular physique. His hair was tied in a topknot that resembled a brush, and he wore a moustache and goatee beard. Below the hem of his straw rain-cloak, the samurai's clothes were drenched. "Sake!" he bellowed. "Someone bring me sake!"

The man was clearly drunk, and the realization sent a wave of disapproval surging through Jimmu.

A samurai should never let himself be seen in public in that state, he thought.

The one-eyed gambler evidently had a different opinion. "Hey, no need to shout," he said to the samurai. "If you want sake, you can help us to finish this bottle, and then we'll order another."

The samurai unfastened his rain-cloak and let it fall to the floor. "Thanks, I will!" he said. "It makes a change to see some friendly faces."

If he thinks those faces are friendly, he must be more drunk than he looks, Jimmu said to himself.

The samurai joined the gamblers, and began to drink and game with them. The potboy brought bottle after bottle of sake, and the play turned rowdy, but

Jimmu sensed an underlying tension, and he noticed how the one-eyed man kept topping up the samurai's sake cup, making sure that he got most of the wine.

Alcohol slowly altered the samurai's mood from amiable to resentful. When the potboy delivered the fifth bottle of sake to the gamblers' table, the samurai lumbered to his feet and stood swaying slightly. "Don't think I don't see what you're up to!" he spluttered. "You're cheating me!"

The one-eyed man stood up, and spoke quickly in a smooth voice. "Calm down, friend! No one's up to anything. You've just had a bit too much sake, that's all. What say we step outside for some fresh air?"

The samurai took a staggering step, and almost lost his balance. The one-eyed man threw an arm around his shoulders to steady him. "Easy, friend!" he said. "You lean on me. I'll help you." He steered the samurai across the inn, and through the front door.

A few seconds later, the other three gamblers abandoned their game, and went outside.

Jimmu paused for a moment, and then went after them; it seemed that real trouble had found him after all.

*

The worst of the storm was over, but rain still fell steadily. In the darkness to Jimmu's right, a scuffle was taking place. The gamblers, armed with daggers, had encircled the samurai, and they jeered as they jabbed at him. The samurai slashed wildly with his sword to keep them away.

Under normal conditions, Jimmu guessed, the samurai would have been more than a match for his assailants, but he was fuddled with sake, and moving clumsily. It was only a matter of time before he dropped his guard, and the gamblers cut him down.

Jimmu did not hesitate. His feet splashed through puddles as he raced across the yard, and his right hand swept his sword from its sheath. His reflexes were so quick that time seemed to slow down. The steel of his sword glinted as he struck with deadly precision. His first blow sliced through the neck of one of the attackers, severing vital arteries; the second blow cleaved through the skull of another man.

The two surviving gamblers panicked, and fled into the night.

"Cowards!" hissed Jimmu. "I've met with robbers

like them before. They hunt in packs, and prey on solitary travellers." He looked at the samurai. "Are you all right?"

The samurai stood with his arms slack at his sides. His shoulders were slumped. He was weeping, the tears mixing with the raindrops that trickled down his face. To Jimmu's total astonishment, the samurai proceeded to recite a poem:

"*The worm in the soil,*
The blind mole in its tunnel,
The man in despair."

"And are you a man in despair?" Jimmu asked.

The samurai sheathed his sword, pressed the palms of his hands together, and bowed. "Please forgive my rudeness," he said. "Sake has made me forget how to behave properly. My name is Yasuda Ryu. Thank you for saving my life – even though it's not worth saving."

The samurai was intriguing, and Jimmu was curious to learn more about him, but not in the yard of an inn on a rainy night. "Come back inside, Yasuda Ryu," he said. "You need to rest."

"I need more than rest!" muttered Ryu, but he did as Jimmu had suggested.

Chapter 4

5TH DAY, 5TH MONTH, 1575

Nobu, the potboy and the stableman had gathered in the doorway of the inn to watch the fight. They stood aside to let Jimmu and Ryu pass.

"My heart rejoices that you're both safe, honoured sirs!" said Nobu. "I had no idea that those men were murdering thieves. You can't trust anyone nowadays. Potboy, carry their miserable carcasses out of the yard!"

The potboy scowled, and nodded in the direction of the stableman. "They're lying closer to the stables than the kitchen," he grumbled. "By rights, *he* ought to deal with them."

A row broke out.

Jimmu and Ryu left the inn staff to their discussion, and seated themselves at Jimmu's table. Ryu stared hard at Jimmu, and struggled to keep his eyes in focus. "What did you say your name was?" he said.

"I didn't. It's Jimmu," said Jimmu.

"And what's the name of your clan?" Ryu asked.

Jimmu was cautious. Although he had felt honour-bound to go to Ryu's assistance, he had no wish to become a close acquaintance. "I don't belong to any clan," he said, hoping that Ryu would take the shortness of his answer as a hint to leave him alone; but his words had the opposite effect.

An absent expression came into Ryu's eyes. "So, we're both outcasts!" he murmured. "I served the same lord for twenty years. Last winter he died unexpectedly, and his son took over as clan leader. I heard rumours that the son had given his father poison, but I thought it was just gossip. A month ago, the new lord told me my services were no longer needed, and that I had to make way for a younger man." Ryu's voice grew hoarse with rage and humiliation. "He gave me some money, and discarded me like a soiled loincloth." Ryu reached inside his kimono, took out a draw-purse, and flung it onto the table. "That's what I got for twenty years of loyalty!"

Jimmu could not keep himself from getting caught up in Ryu's story. "Did you do something to offend your lord?" he said.

"He made a secret alliance with his father's bitterest enemy," said Ryu. "I found out by accident, and questioned the wisdom of His Lordship's action."

"A samurai should obey without question," said Jimmu, and immediately felt ashamed. What right did he have to pass judgement on Yasuda Ryu, when he himself was guilty of disobedience to his master?

Ryu laughed bitterly. "You're young," he said. "You believe that things are either good or evil. But what if they're a mixture of the two? What if a lord issues a samurai with a dishonourable order? Should the samurai obey it?"

"A samurai and his lord should share the same sense of honour," said Jimmu.

"The new lord and I share nothing," Ryu said. "He wishes to be a great lord, not through showing courage and skill in battle, but by scheming, and playing politics." Ryu hiccupped and belched. "But I have schemes of my own. I mean to be revenged on Hiki Sabura."

Jimmu was so astounded that he almost cried out, but his astonishment quickly turned into suspicion. Was it sheer coincidence that had brought him and Ryu together at The Fortunate Swallows, or was something more sinister going on? He decided to play along until he could be sure. "Revenge?" he said.

Ryu leaned across the table. His face was so close to Jimmu's that Jimmu could smell the sake on his breath.

"I wasn't always a samurai, you know," Ryu confided. "When I was younger, I was trained to be a ninja."

Jimmu knew dozens of stories about ninja. They were mysterious warriors, skilled spies and assassins who hired themselves out to anyone who could afford their price. In most of the stories Jimmu had heard, ninja were credited with supernatural powers: they could fly, and walk on water; they evaded their enemies by turning themselves into animals, or plants, or shadows. Ryu did not look as if he had any supernatural powers; perhaps the sake was making him brag.

"Is this a joke, Yasuda Ryu?" asked Jimmu.

"No joke," Ryu assured him. "I was raised in a

ninja village, in Iga Province. My parents died when I was a baby, and my uncle adopted me. My cousin Ichiro and I grew up together, and we were like brothers. We were both trained by a master ninja named Goro. Then..." Ryu shrugged with one shoulder. "Ichiro and I had a disagreement. I left my village and became a samurai instead of a ninja. I haven't seen Ichiro and Goro for years, but I'm going to get back in touch with them, and put some ninja work their way. I'll use Lord Sabura's money to hire them."

"You're going to pay them to murder him?" said Jimmu.

"D'you take me for a coward?" Ryu retorted. "I want them to break into His Lordship's castle, and steal his private papers. I'm counting on finding something among them that I can take to the Emperor, something that will shame Lord Sabura in the same way that he shamed me."

Ryu slumped back and yawned. "I must go to bed," he said. "Forgive the way I rambled on. I shouldn't drink sake, it loosens my tongue. Sleep well, Jimmu."

"And you," Jimmu said.

*

Later that night, Jimmu lay in the dark, listening to the wind and rain outside, and the snores of Ryu and the plump man. Jimmu's mind was spinning like a millstone, grinding out thoughts and questions.

His plan, if it could be called a plan, had been to ride to Tokoro Castle, and attempt to rescue Takeko by himself; an honourable course of action, but one that offered only a slender chance of success. Now he saw another possibility. With the help of Ryu and a few ninja, he might have a real chance of freeing Takeko and returning her to her father.

But would it be right? Samurai warriors considered ninja beneath contempt, common criminals who fought for money, not honour. If Jimmu joined forces with them, would he be going against the Samurai Code?

Jimmu closed his right hand around the jade horse at his neck, and a recollection of Takeko suddenly came to him. One winter's night, they had met in the garden of Mitsukage Castle. He remembered her walking towards him through falling snow, white flakes catching in her dark hair, and the memory of her beauty made him long to see her again.

The memory became a dream as he drifted off to sleep.

In the honoured guests' room at Tokoro Castle, Takeko was preparing for bed. Aki, the maidservant Lord Sabura had provided for her, helped her to undress and put on her night shift, then unpinned her hair and combed it. Takeko usually found it soothing; Aki was the only person who had shown her genuine consideration since her imprisonment. Tonight, however, Aki was distracted, and her hands had lost their usual gentleness.

"What's wrong, Aki?" Takeko asked.

Aki stopped combing, sat back on her heels, and looked down at the floor. "I can't say, My Lady," she said. "I don't want to sound disloyal to Lord Sabura."

Takeko smiled. "Be honest with me," she said. "Any conversation we have is just between ourselves. You can be as disloyal as you like."

Aki spoke hesitantly, in a voice that barely rose

above a whisper. "When I was a little girl, a bird catcher used to come to my village, selling songbirds in cages. He poked them with a stick to make them sing. I felt sorry for those birds. They belonged in the sky, not in cages. I wished I had the money to buy them all, and set them free." Aki lifted her head. "I think about those birds whenever I'm with you, My Lady. This room is your cage, and Lord Sabura is like the cruel bird catcher. I wish there was something I could do to help you."

For the first time in days, Takeko dared to hope. "Do you really mean that?" she asked.

"Of course, My Lady."

Takeko thought quickly. "Get up for a moment, Aki," she said.

The two young women stood face to face.

"We're almost the same size," Takeko said. "If I were to dress in your clothes..."

Aki was shocked by the idea. "My Lady?" she gasped.

"Haven't I seen you wearing a hat with a veil?" asked Takeko.

"Yes, My Lady," Aki said. "If I don't keep my face

covered, some of His Lordship's guards make improper remarks when I go past them."

"Perfect!" exclaimed Takeko.

Aki frowned. "What's perfect, My Lady? I don't understand."

Takeko sketched out her plan simply, so that Aki would be able to follow it. "Suppose you came to me early one morning, wearing your veiled hat," she said. "If you gave me your clothes, I could put them on, pull down the veil, and pretend to be you. Then I could leave the castle when the guards lower the drawbridge."

Aki flinched. "But Lord Sabura would be angry, My Lady!" she protested. "He'd have me tortured and killed."

"Not if you let me tie you up and gag you," said Takeko. "We could scatter things around the room to make it look as if there had been a struggle. You could tell Lord Sabura that I took you by surprise, and overpowered you."

Aki was reluctant. "I don't know, My Lady," she said. "We'd both be taking a terrible risk."

"If I manage to escape, you can wait for an

opportunity to slip away, and come to be my maid in Mitsukage Castle," said Takeko. "My father is sure to reward you."

A greedy glint showed in Aki's eyes. "What kind of reward, My Lady?" she said.

It was dark when Jimmu woke. Moving quietly, so as not to disturb the other sleeping guests, he left his bed, and went out into a meadow behind the inn. Here he sat cross-legged, with his hands resting on his knees, breathing in deeply as he prepared to meditate. He had important choices to make, and needed to think clearly.

A thin mist hung over the meadow. The eastern sky was growing light, and birdsong spread out in every direction as the dawn chorus began.

Jimmu composed himself, and cleared his mind of all distractions. His sense of self slowly dissolved until he had no identity, and was as much a part of his surroundings as the grass in the meadow, and the vanishing mist.

When Jimmu finished meditating, the sun was up,

and he had made his decision. The night before, he had pondered whether it would be right for him to seek help from a band of ninja. Now he saw that the real problem had been his vanity: he had been afraid of how his fellow samurai might judge him.

But what does my reputation matter, compared with Takeko's safety? he asked himself.

Jimmu was not sure how far he should trust Ryu, but for the moment their interests seemed to coincide. He would tell Yasuda Ryu about Takeko, and go with him to the ninja to ask for their assistance in freeing her.

Jimmu got to his feet, and returned to The Fortunate Swallows. The plump man was awake, and was rubbing his eyes and scratching himself. There was no sign of Ryu.

"Where's the samurai?" Jimmu asked the plump man.

"How would I know?" the man answered. "He must have left while I was asleep."

"Just after sunrise, to be precise," said a voice.

Jimmu turned, and saw Nobu standing in the doorway of the back room.

"You'll be happy to learn that your friend was

generous enough to settle your bill, as well as his own," said Nobu.

"Did he mention where he was going?" Jimmu asked.

"No, but he rode off in the direction of the Kyoto Road," said Nobu. "Would you like the potboy to serve you some food?"

Jimmu left the question unanswered, and hurried outside to the stables.

There was heavy traffic on the Kyoto Road. Carts loaded with produce trundled along behind mule trains carrying bales of silk and sacks of spices. Poorer traders bent under the weight of their packs. Here and there, mounted samurai cleared the way for dignitaries in covered litters. Almost all the traffic was headed in the same direction, towards Kyoto, the Imperial City.

Jimmu could not pick out Ryu among the crowds on the road, and he made slow progress. He felt frustrated, and angry with himself for letting his best chance of rescuing Takeko slip away.

By noon, the heat was oppressive. Jimmu had

almost given up hope, when he spotted a lone horseman leave the main road for a side road up ahead. It was impossible to make out the man's face in the shimmering air, but he was approximately the same height and build as Ryu, and when Jimmu reached the side road, he turned off the Kyoto Road. Before long, he reached a grove of trees. A stream ran beside the grove, and a horse was drinking from it; Ryu stood beside the horse.

Ryu was not pleased to see Jimmu. "You again?" he rasped. "Why did you follow me? What d'you want?"

Jimmu dismounted, and led the mare to the stream. "Last night, you spoke to me about ninja," he said. "Were you telling the truth?"

"Go away! Leave me alone!" growled Ryu. "Forget what I said last night. I was drunk."

"Because if what you told me is true, I know a better way for you to be revenged on Hiki Sabura," Jimmu said.

"And what makes my revenge any of your business?" demanded Ryu.

Jimmu told Ryu about Takeko, Lord Ankan and

Lord Sabura; Ryu tugged thoughtfully at his goatee while he listened.

"I intended to attack Tokoro Castle single-handed—" said Jimmu.

"That would be suicide!" Ryu broke in.

"I admit that my chances of rescuing Lady Takeko on my own are slim," said Jimmu. "But if I had you and your ninja friends with me, I might be able to free her."

"Ah!" said Ryu.

"When the dragon strikes
The soldier and the tiger
Battle side by side."

Jimmu grasped the point of the poem at once. "Will you join forces with me, Yasuda Ryu?" he said. "Shall we go into battle side by side?"

Ryu paced back and forth, mumbling to himself and gesturing, as if he were arguing with someone invisible. At last, he placed his hands on his hips and faced Jimmu. "All right," he said. "But I'm only agreeing because I owe you for last night, and I know that if I don't agree, you'll go to Tokoro alone, and get yourself killed."

"The true samurai must arrange the best death he can," said Jimmu.

"Agreed, but the *sensible* samurai doesn't just throw his life away," Ryu countered. He chuckled. "I have to admit that I like this idea of yours more and more. Spoiling one of Lord Sabura's dirty little schemes really appeals to me."

"How long will it take us to get to your village in Iga?" asked Jimmu.

"Goro and Ichiro won't be in Iga," Ryu said. "Goro likes to travel around in the late spring, gathering information and looking for business. Ichiro, his wife Yuki, and Goro put on puppet shows as a front. I've been tracking them. They're somewhere here in Ise Province."

"How will we find them?" asked Jimmu. "There are scores of puppet troupes working in Ise at this time of year."

"They don't all have blind storytellers though," Ryu said. He grinned at Jimmu's puzzled expression. "Goro has been blind since birth."

Jimmu was aghast. "I'm going to a blind man for help?" he muttered.

"Don't underestimate Goro," Ryu warned. "His blindness didn't stop him from becoming a great master ninja. He's more skilled as a fighter than most of the samurai I've come across.

Diamonds and silk

Here within my sake cup

I hold the night sky."

"What does that mean?" said Jimmu.

"It means that things aren't always what they seem," Ryu explained.

"Where d'you get these poems of yours, Ryu?" asked Jimmu.

"I make them up," Ryu replied. "I'm thinking of becoming a poet when I'm an old man — if I live to be an old man, that is."

Jimmu shook his head. He had entered a shadowy world where puppeteers were assassins, blind men were skilled warriors, and samurai were poets.

Nothing was certain.

Lord Sabura and Takeko were in the reception room of Tokoro Castle. The walls were hung with calligraphy scrolls; a white porcelain vase containing a sprig of blossom stood in an alcove; a screen door had been moved aside to give a view of the castle's garden.

Lord Sabura was listening to the ringing of a set of wind chimes that hung in the doorway. "The air smells of summer today," he said. "I detect the odours of freshly cut grass, and late lilac. The summer is an unpleasant time. The sunlight is too harsh, and the heat can be suffocating. I far prefer winter – the silhouette of bare branches against the sky, the whiteness of snow. Which is your favourite season, Takeko?"

"I don't have one, My Lord," said Takeko.

Lord Sabura's nostrils flared. "I have asked you before to call me by my name, Takeko, and I wish that you would. It is not as if you were a servant!"

"I'll try to remember, Sabura," said Takeko.

Lord Sabura rearranged the sleeves of his kimono. "I have received more news of young Jimmu," he said casually. "It seems he has left Mitsukage Castle, and incurred your father's displeasure."

Takeko started. "Why did Jimmu leave Mitsukage? Did he argue with my father?"

"Who knows?" replied Lord Sabura. "Perhaps Jimmu is going to attempt a heroic rescue of you, and intends to storm the castle single-handed?"

"He wouldn't be so foolish!" Takeko said.

"No?" said Lord Sabura. "Forgive me, Takeko, but when you talked of Jimmu on a previous occasion, I sensed that there was a special bond between the two of you."

"How could there be?" Takeko exclaimed. "He is a samurai, and I'm a noblewoman."

"You were *born* a noblewoman, but you do not *behave* as other noblewomen do," said Lord Sabura. "You are beautiful, but you do not use your beauty to beguile. You speak your mind, and you have a formidable temper. I think you enjoy defying convention, Takeko – is it not so?"

Takeko was silent; she knew that Lord Sabura was testing her, probing for new ways to cause her pain.

Lord Sabura spread his hands. "The noble samurai, sacrificing himself for the woman he loves, even though their love cannot be. What a romantic tale!"

"Why don't you write it?" suggested Takeko.

"Prose is too crude," Lord Sabura said. "Poetry is

more to my liking." He smiled. "In a strange way, you and I are similar, Takeko. We are both rebels. You are not like other women, and I understand you because I am not like other men."

"That's true, Sabura," said Takeko. "You're not like other men."

Lord Sabura smiled knowingly. "You are being sarcastic with me, Takeko, but before long you will learn that what you just said is true," he said. "Other men's intelligence is inferior to my own."

Takeko suspected that Lord Sabura was planning something, and dreaded what it might be.

Chapter 6
6TH DAY, 5TH MONTH, 1575

Jimmu and Ryu rejoined the Kyoto Road, and Ryu explained the thinking behind his method of searching for the puppeteer-ninja. "This road is always busy," he said. "It has the biggest inns with the biggest audiences for wandering entertainers. We'll stop at some of the inns, and ask if Goro and the others have been there recently."

"Isn't there a quicker way?" asked Jimmu. "At the end of the month, Lord Ankan will march his soldiers out of Mitsukage Castle, and when he does—"

"We're doing all we can, Jimmu," Ryu said. "You'll have to be patient." He lifted a hand to his chin, and pulled at his goatee. "Something's been puzzling me about you. You're courageous, and a good fighter. Why would Choju Ankan waste a promising samurai by sending him on a suicide mission?"

Jimmu blushed. "Lord Ankan didn't send me," he confessed. "I left Mitsukage against his wishes."

"Now I'm even more puzzled!" exclaimed Ryu. "You follow the Samurai Code, and yet you disobeyed your lord – why?"

Jimmu's blush grew hotter. "As far as Lord Ankan is concerned, his daughter is already dead," he said. "His grief is terrible. I wanted to try and ease his suffering."

"And how would dying at Tokoro have done that?" said Ryu. "You don't strike me as a fool, Jimmu. What's the real reason behind all this?"

Jimmu squirmed in his saddle. "Lady Takeko is a brave young woman. She doesn't deserve to die at the hands of a coward."

"A-a-h!" Ryu said knowingly. "Is Lady Takeko also very beautiful, by any chance?"

"She's My Lord's daughter," said Jimmu. "I've never considered whether she's beautiful or not. A true samurai doesn't concern himself with such things."

Ryu laughed. "Then it's strange how many samurai marry, and have children!" he said. "Remember, a samurai is only human, and no human is perfect. We all have flaws."

Jimmu was all too aware of the wisdom of Ryu's words.

They called at three inns, but no one could tell them anything about puppeteers. Late that afternoon, they rode into the courtyard of The Lucky Dragon, a fine inn that looked as though it charged high prices.

Two geisha girls came out onto the veranda. The geisha were pretty, and wore fashionable kimonos.

"Good day, handsome strangers!" said the taller of the girls. "I'm Airi, and my companion is Chou. Won't you come inside with us, and take some refreshment?"

Chou hid a well-rehearsed shy smile behind her fan, and peeped over the top at Jimmu. Her gaze made him feel self-conscious, and embarrassed. "We only want information," he said brusquely. "Have any puppeteers passed through here?"

"Not since last autumn," said Airi. "But last night, one of our guests spoke about a puppet show that he saw in the village of Izumison not long ago. He claimed the puppeteers were the cleverest he'd seen."

"He was particularly impressed by their blind storyteller," Chou added.

Jimmu narrowed his eyes. "When was this?" he barked. "Bring the guest here, so we can talk to him!"

Airi was taken aback by Jimmu's aggressiveness. "Unfortunately, he left early this morning," she said.

Jimmu cursed.

"Forgive my friend's hastiness, ladies," Ryu said. "One of the puppeteers stole something from him, and he's anxious to get it back."

"If your friend is troubled in spirit, let Chou and me soothe him with our singing and dancing," said Airi.

Ryu bowed. "Tempting though your offer is, ladies, I'm afraid that we must be leaving. Another time, perhaps."

As they rode back to the Kyoto Road, Ryu scolded Jimmu. "What's the matter with you?" he said. "Why were you rude to those geisha? Would it have done you any harm to speak to them politely?"

"I never know what to say to women," said Jimmu. "They confuse me."

"Especially when they're young and pretty, eh?" Ryu teased. "We'll have to find a farmhouse where we can buy supplies. I know a few short cuts we can use, but Izumison is still a long hard ride from here."

"How can you be sure that the puppeteers the geisha talked about are the ones we're looking for?" asked Jimmu.

"Because it makes sense," Ryu said. "Izumison isn't far from the High Road to the north. If they're heading back to Iga, that's the most direct route."

The sun was setting. Many of the travellers had left the Kyoto Road to seek lodgings for the night, and the traffic was far lighter now. Ryu pointed out a drover's trail that branched off to the right, and the two samurai were about to join it when they heard a sudden commotion behind them. Jimmu wheeled his horse round to investigate.

Five mounted soldiers in armour were bearing down on him at full gallop. A shout carried above the drumming of the horses' hooves. "You two! Stay where you are!"

As the soldiers drew closer, Jimmu saw that two of them wore flags fitted to the back plate of their armour that carried the emblem of the Hiki Clan, three white squares on a dark blue background. Within a few seconds, the soldiers had enclosed Jimmu and Ryu in a circle.

Jimmu identified the soldiers' leader, a round-faced man whose fleshy neck bulged over the chinstrap of his helmet. He had an authority about him, and also the air of someone who was pleased with himself. "I knew it would be you, Yasuda Ryu," he said. "The landlord of The Fortunate Swallows described you perfectly. I haven't seen you at Tokoro for a while. Where have you been?"

"Here and there, Sergeant Hayato," Ryu replied. "Lord Sabura and I had a difference of opinion, and we both agreed that I should find a position elsewhere."

While this exchange was taking place, Jimmu watched carefully and readied himself for action, looking out for the slightest opening that might give him an advantage if things turned ugly. One of the soldiers was sweating profusely, and he blinked rapidly as the sweat ran into his eyes. Sergeant Hayato's mount was being troubled by a horsefly, and kept twitching its head. The sergeant had to struggle to keep the animal under control.

Sergeant Hayato turned to Jimmu. "And you must be Jimmu, Choju Ankan's man," he said. "Nobu heard Ryu mention your name last night. Lord Sabura is eager to meet you, Jimmu. He's sent out search parties for you."

"There must have been a misunderstanding, Sergeant Hayato!" Ryu insisted. "This man doesn't have anything to do with Choju Ankan. He's Yasuda Jimmu, my nephew from Shikoku. I'm taking him to Kyoto to show him the sights."

Sergeant Hayato frowned briefly, and then shook his head in grudging admiration. "You're the biggest and best liar I ever met, Ryu, but it won't work this time. You're free to go, I'm not interested in you. I advise you to ride away, and leave Jimmu to us."

At that instant, the horsefly stung Sergeant Hayato's steed on its rump. The horse whinnied, bucked and reared, startling the other horses in the circle.

The momentary confusion was all that Jimmu needed. He drew his sword, moved his mare forwards, stood up in his stirrups, and struck Sergeant Hayato with a cut known as "priest's robe", slicing off the sergeant's head, right arm and shoulder. Twisting in his saddle, Jimmu brought his sword up and across, slashing open the stomach of the soldier to Sergeant Hayato's left.

Another of the soldiers charged at Jimmu, drawing a long sword specially made for use on horseback, but the man was too slow. He was still raising the weapon above his head when the point of Jimmu's blade drove into his heart. Ryu dispatched the remaining two soldiers effortlessly.

And then there was no more fighting, just dead men on the ground, and riderless horses galloping away. The air stank of death; blowflies had already settled on the corpses.

Jimmu glanced over at Ryu, who was cleaning his sword with a piece of cloth. Ryu had blood on his face from the men he had killed. He closed his eyes, and chanted:

"*Wind in the branches*
Dry whispering of barley
Ghosts of the fallen."

Ryu opened his eyes and grinned. "It looks as if I've

definitely left Lord Sabura's service now, doesn't it?" he said.

"I don't understand!" said Jimmu. "What does Hiki Sabura want with me?"

"I've no idea," Ryu said, "but I suggest that we don't wait around here to find out."

The second day of their journey to Izumison passed without incident. On the third night, Jimmu and Ryu made camp near the ruins of a drover's hut at the side of the trail. They watered their horses at a brook, rolled their sleeping mats out on the ground and sat on them, eating the rice cakes they had bought from a farmer's wife the day before.

The fight on the Kyoto Road had created a bond between Jimmu and Ryu, and since then Jimmu had got to know his companion a little better. Ryu was an odd mixture. At times he was excellent company, telling jokes and composing poems to cheer Jimmu up; at other times Ryu brooded, and Jimmu sensed that something was troubling him.

That night, Ryu seemed at his lowest, staring at nothing, and sighing.

At first, Jimmu thought it would be better to leave Ryu alone, but Ryu's silence went on for so long that it began to seem sinister, and Jimmu could not resist the impulse to break it. "I don't mean to pry, Ryu," he said, "but have I done something to offend you?"

"Offend me?" said Ryu. "No. Why d'you ask?"

"You're so quiet."

Ryu washed down the last of a rice cake with a swig of water from his canteen, and wiped his mouth with the back of his hand. "Sometimes," he said falteringly, "after you decide to do something for what you *think* is a good reason, it turns out that—" Ryu broke off with a grunt. "Remember I told you that I grew up with my cousin Ichiro?"

Jimmu nodded. "You said the two of you were like brothers."

"Do you have brothers, Jimmu?" asked Ryu.

"No," Jimmu said. "I was an only child."

"Brothers aren't always close and loving," said Ryu. "They often squabble, and try to outdo each other. Ichiro and I were like that. I was jealous of him because my uncle and aunt paid more attention to him than they did to me. When we were young, we both fell in love with the same girl, Yuki. She chose to marry Ichiro, not me." Ryu's voice became hoarse with emotion. "I behaved like a fool. I lost my temper and challenged Ichiro to a duel, but he refused to fight me. He was so calm that it made me ashamed of myself. I left my village and never went back."

Jimmu waited a few seconds before he spoke again. "Two samurai cannot be close friends until they see into each other's hearts," he said. "Thank you for letting me see into yours, Ryu."

Ryu waved dismissively. "I was like you once," he said. "I believed that if I dedicated myself to the Samurai Code, it would solve all life's problems. If only life were that straightforward..." He chuckled. "Listen to me! I sound like an old man lecturing his grandchildren. Let's sleep. We should get to Izumison by tomorrow afternoon. And a good thing too – those rice cakes are going stale."

Jimmu lay on his back and looked up at the stars. A thought kept nagging at him: Ryu had admitted a secret, but he had offered nothing in return. "Ryu?" he said softly. "When I left Mitsukage Castle to go on a warrior pilgrimage two years ago, I thought I was in love with Lady Takeko, and I thought she was in love with me."

Ryu replied with a loud snore.

The following afternoon, the two samurai rode into Izumison. The inn there – The Amusing Wonder – was easy to find, as it was the largest building in the village.

The landlady was a widow named Chika. Her face broke into a buck-toothed smile when Jimmu asked her about the puppeteers. "They were wonderful!" she said. "The old blind man knows how to spin a yarn, and the flute player had the customers weeping into their sake cups. The boy was excellent too."

"Boy?" said Ryu.

"A pretty lad, about sixteen or seventeen," said Chika. "He didn't talk much, but when he handled a puppet, you'd swear it had come to life. They were here for five days. I wanted them to stay longer because they were so good for business, but they left early this morning."

"Did they say where they were going?" said Jimmu.

"No," Chika said, "but I saw their ox cart on the High Road."

"It's as I thought, Jimmu, they're making for Iga," said Ryu.

Chika rolled her eyes. "Iga – why Iga?" she hooted. "There's nothing in Iga Province except mountains and bandits! I told them they'd earn a fortune in Kyoto, but they didn't seem interested. Artistic types aren't bothered about money. Now you must excuse me, gentlemen, I have bills to collect. If you want to stay here, ask one of the servants. My prices are very reasonable."

"Thank you, landlady, but we have other plans," Jimmu said with a bow.

Chika scratched her chin. "Why would two samurai be looking for a troupe of puppeteers, I wonder?" she said.

"Our master knows the reputation of the troupe who played at your inn, and sent us to find them," said Ryu. "His youngest son is to be married, and he wants a puppet show to form part of the wedding celebration."

Jimmu was surprised at how smoothly Ryu lied,

and when they were outside the inn, he complimented Ryu on his quick-wittedness.

"It's a habit of mine," Ryu said. "Never let your enemies know your plans. Mislead them with false information." His expression suddenly changed; he cursed, and slapped his forehead. "Wait here, Jimmu!" he muttered. "I won't be long."

Ryu went back inside. Through the open door, Jimmu saw him approach Chika. He put his mouth close to her ear, and said something as he slipped her a few coins. Chika smiled, and nodded. Ryu left her, and returned to Jimmu.

"What did you say to her?" Jimmu asked.

"I remembered that while we were talking to her, I was stupid enough to call you by name," said Ryu. "I told her that if any soldiers came asking after you, she was to say nothing."

"D'you think Lord Sabura would send search parties this far north?" Jimmu said.

Ryu shrugged, and changed the subject. "So, Goro, Ichiro and Yuki have a boy with them?" he said. "I wonder who he is? Probably a pupil of Goro's. Only one way to find out – let's get after them!"

*

The High Road to the north was not as well kept as the road to Kyoto. The ground was still muddy from the recent storm, and churned up by traffic. Ryu searched for telltale signs of a trail that Jimmu was unable to see. At a spot where the road was joined by a path that led to a farmhouse, Ryu stopped, and pointed. "An ox wagon came through here," he said. "Look at the deep ruts its wheels made! And over there, where the grass is flattened, someone pushing a handcart stood aside to let the wagon pass."

Jimmu was impressed. "Who taught you how to track, Ryu?" he asked.

"I learned when I was a child," Ryu answered. "Tracking is a useful skill for a ninja." He turned his gaze back to the mud. "There are two riders with the wagon. One of the horses is smaller and lighter than the other. Its hoofs have left shallower prints."

"Could it be the boy?" said Jimmu.

"Almost certainly," Ryu said. "The other rider will be Ichiro. We'll have to be careful. If Goro knows he's being followed, he might be lying in ambush somewhere."

"How could he know?" asked Jimmu.

"Ninja are cautious," Ryu replied. "It wouldn't take long for the boy to climb a tree, and look back along the road. Let me take the lead. Ichiro is a fine archer, and you're a stranger to him. He might still recognize me, even after all these years."

"We should ride shoulder to shoulder, like brother samurai," said Jimmu.

Ryu hauled himself onto his saddle. "This is no time for noble gestures, Jimmu!" he said. "In the old chronicles, samurai are always high-minded and honourable. In real life, honour is a more complex matter. Age has taught me to make compromises."

"A true samurai would never compromise his honour!" declared Jimmu.

"Then perhaps I wasn't a true samurai, which explains why I'm here with you, instead of carrying out my duties at Tokoro," Ryu said. "Forget your objections, and let me ride in front, Jimmu. Remember our conversation in The Fortunate Swallows? If you want to save Lady Takeko, you have to stay alive."

*

The afternoon grew hotter, and the air felt thick and heavy. The farms alongside the road became more and more isolated until they finally petered out altogether, leaving Jimmu and Ryu in wild country.

The heat made Jimmu drowsy, and he had to struggle to keep his eyes open. He could no longer tell if he was actually riding, or if he was asleep and dreaming about it.

An urgent hiss from Ryu brought him fully awake. "Stop!"

"What is it, Ryu?" said Jimmu.

"There!"

Directly ahead, the road ran into woodland. Two lines of fir trees cast shadows that formed a black tunnel.

"A good place for an ambush," said Ryu. "When we ride into the shadows, it'll take our eyes a few seconds to adjust, and we'll be at a disadvantage."

The hairs on the back of Jimmu's neck prickled. Somewhere in the gloom, an archer might be taking aim. Which of them would he shoot at first?

"What shall we do?" Jimmu whispered.

Ryu's response was bizarre; he threw back his head, and sang raucously:

"Wherever I look,

The cherry blossom is as thick as clouds.

Next year when the cherry flowers,

I'll be with my love in Iga."

And suddenly a man was standing on the road, at the mouth of the tunnel.

Jimmu gasped: he had seen no movement; the man was simply there, as if he had dropped out of the sky.

The man was old, with long white hair tied back in a braid. His skin was the colour of parchment, and his face was wrinkled. He had a sharp nose like a bird's beak; a milky film covered both his eyes. His hands grasped a staff. The sleeves of his cotton jerkin had fallen back, exposing his bony wrists and forearms. "Your singing hasn't improved, Yasuda Ryu," he said, "but at least you can still remember the signal song."

Ryu bowed respectfully. "It's good to see you again, master."

The old man winced. "I haven't been your master for many years," he said. "You're old enough to call me by name."

"As you wish, Goro," said Ryu.

Jimmu blinked rapidly. *This* was Goro, a ninja

master? Jimmu had expected a giant, with muscles like a sumo wrestler's, not a scrawny monkey. What use would he be in rescuing Takeko?

Jimmu's spirits sank. He should not have listened to Ryu, or built up his hopes. His mission had failed before it had properly begun.

Takeko was going to die.

Chapter 8

Another man stepped out of the shadow-tunnel, and stood beside Goro. He was handsome, with deep-set eyes and a square chin. Two broad grey streaks in his hair gave him the look of a badger. His clothes were black. He held a bow, and though his grip on it appeared casual, Jimmu noticed that he kept two fingers closed over the shaft of the arrow notched to his bowstring. Ryu and the man stared at each other.

"You look well, Ichiro," said Ryu.

Ichiro scowled. "What d'you want, Ryu?" he demanded. "Are you planning to betray us to a troop of your lord's soldiers?"

Jimmu felt a wave of hostility pass between the two men, and interrupted their conversation before a fight broke out. "Yasuda Ryu brought me to you because we need your help," he explained.

Goro cocked his head in Jimmu's direction. "And who are you, young samurai?" he said.

"My name is Jimmu," said Jimmu. "I serve—"

"Lord Choju Ankan," Goro said. "I've heard of you."

Jimmu was surprised. "How can that be?" he said.

Goro smiled. "Some people talk, others listen and repeat what they've been told. Why do you need my help?"

Jimmu's instinct told him to be direct. "Lord Hiki Sabura has allied himself with the Takeda Clan," he said. "He's holding Lord Ankan's daughter, Lady Takeko, prisoner. Lord Oda Nobunaga will not let Lord Ankan attack Lord Sabura. At the end of the month, Lord Ankan will send reinforcements to Lord Nobunaga. When he does, Lady Takeko will be put to death. I need your help to save her."

Goro pursed his lips. "Interesting!" he said. "And since Lord Ankan would never lower himself to employ ninja, I presume that you're acting without his approval?"

"You presume correctly," said Jimmu.

"I usually do," Goro said. "What's your part in this, Ryu?"

Ryu's reply was as frank as Jimmu's had been. "I want revenge," he said. "Lord Sabura paid me off. He said I was too old-fashioned to be of use to him. He insulted me, and I mean to pay him back for it."

"So!" said Goro. "We have one samurai with a grudge against his lord, and another who wants to rescue his lord's daughter without his lord's consent. What do you think, Ichiro?"

"I don't trust them," Ichiro said.

Goro tutted. "Don't be hasty, Ichiro! I want to learn more, but I'm hungry. Let's get out of the sun, and have something to eat. I think better on a full stomach."

The ninja's wagon was concealed behind a stand of bamboo. It was an unusual vehicle, with tall sides made from planks of wood. The back had been boarded up and fitted with a small door. Sacking had been stretched over hoops to form a roof. The oxen were still in their traces, and were feeding from nosebags.

A woman was standing beside the wagon. She was striking-looking, with high cheekbones and a wide mouth.

"We have guests, Yuki!" Goro called to her. "The young man's name is Jimmu. You already know his companion."

Ryu gazed at Yuki, then remembered his manners, and bowed. "You haven't changed, Yuki," he said.

"Of course I've changed!" retorted Yuki. "I was still a girl when you last saw me. I'm a grown woman now."

"To me, you will always be—" Ryu began to say.

"We can talk about the past later," Goro broke in. "Where is Ren?"

"Watering the horses," said Yuki.

"Would you be so kind as to prepare a meal for our visitors and ourselves?" Goro said. "Ichiro and Ryu will help by gathering firewood."

Ichiro and Ryu exchanged unfriendly glances.

Yuki frowned. "Are you sure that's wise, Goro?"

"Quite sure," said Goro. "They'll set aside their old differences and work together, because I'm telling them to. Jimmu and I need to talk in private. There's a fallen tree somewhere near the wagon, Jimmu. Guide me to it. We can sit down, and rest as we speak."

"I'm happy to stand," Jimmu said.

Goro thumped the butt of his staff on the ground. "But I'm not!" he chided. "Have a little consideration for my age!"

Jimmu led Goro to the tree, and Goro sighed as he lowered himself onto it. "Sit next to me, Jimmu," he said. "Let me touch your face. I want to know what you look like."

Jimmu sat down, and let Goro's fingertips explore his features.

After a few seconds, Goro lowered his hands into his lap. "Ah, yes!" he murmured. "I understand."

"Understand what?" asked Jimmu.

"Pardon my frankness, but three years ago I heard rumours about you and Lady Takeko. It was said that you were a favourite of hers, and that you were fond of each other. Are you still fond of her?"

Jimmu's first impulse was to tell Goro to mind his own business, but once again his instinct told him to be truthful. "I'm still fond of her memory," he said.

"A good answer!" said Goro. "I thought it must be so. It explains why you're so anxious to save Lady Takeko."

Jimmu was startled by the depth of Goro's insight, and tried to mask his alarm. "What makes you think I'm anxious?" he asked, puzzled.

"Because you're risking everything for her," said Goro, "your life, your lord's good opinion, and your reputation. I know what samurai think of ninja. They despise us because we take money for what we do. Great lords secretly employ us as spies, or to get rid of an enemy, but they hate and fear us."

"Why?" said Jimmu. "A great lord is more powerful than a ninja."

"But a ninja is free," Goro said. "He does not owe allegiance to any lord or clan, and can do as he pleases. The great lords' power rests on the obedience of others. They feel threatened by the idea of freedom."

Jimmu was confused. The concept of a free warrior was so alien to everything he had been taught to believe that it repelled him; but he knew he would have to ignore his personal feelings for Takeko's sake.

"Will you help me?" he asked bluntly.

"I'll think it over," Goro promised. "That's enough talking. Let's join the others. I must eat!"

While two guards kept watch, Takeko and Aki sheltered from the sun in the shade of a red-leafed maple tree in the garden of Tokoro Castle, cooling their faces with fans.

"Smile, Aki!" murmured Takeko.

"Why?" said Aki.

"To make the guards think we're sharing gossip," Takeko said.

Aki forced herself to smile.

"Have you thought about the suggestion I made to you?" Takeko asked.

"I haven't been able to think of anything else, My Lady," said Aki. "I want to help you, but the risk terrifies me."

Takeko pretended to laugh. "How can you repeat such things, Aki!" she said loudly, for the benefit of the guards, and then went on in a lower voice. "If I'm thorough there'll be no risk. I'll tie you up tightly, and scratch your face so it looks as if you've been in a fight."

"Scratch my face, My Lady?" gasped Aki.

"Don't worry, I won't leave you scarred," Takeko assured her. "You're the only friend I've got here, Aki. I'm depending on you. Will you do it for me?"

Aki took a deep breath. "Yes, My Lady!" she said.

Chapter 9
9TH DAY, 5TH MONTH, 1575

While Jimmu and Goro had been talking, Ryu and Ichiro had built a fire at a safe distance from the wagon. Flames leaped at the base of a pot suspended from a metal tripod. Yuki was stirring the contents of the pot with a ladle.

Ichiro and Ryu were on opposite sides of the fire. Ryu sat cross-legged with his arms folded. Ichiro lay on his back, gazing up through the branches of the firs.

Two horses were tethered to the back of the wagon. One was a roan; the other was a shaggy pot-bellied animal, not much bigger than a pony. A boy was stroking the muzzle of the shaggy horse as he whispered to it. When he noticed Jimmu and Goro approaching, the boy turned his head.

He was small and lithe. Like Ichiro, he wore black clothes. He was, as the landlady of The Amusing

Wonder had said, a pretty boy, with a snub nose, a small soft mouth, and dark eyes. His hair was drawn up under a straw hat, in a way that emphasized how far his ears stuck out.

Jimmu saluted the boy with a nod. "You must be Ren," he said.

"That's right," said the boy. His voice was light, not yet broken. "And you must be Jimmu. I thought you would be taller."

Jimmu smiled at the boy's unexpected comment. "I'm sorry I don't live up to your expectations," he said.

Goro laughed. "Stop petting that beast of yours, Ren," he scolded. "Go and help Yuki. I hope you enjoy our food, Jimmu. It's bound to taste better than the stale rice cakes you ate this morning."

"How did you know what I ate this morning?" said Jimmu.

"I smelled your breath when we were talking," Goro said. "When you're blind, you depend on your other senses more than sighted people do."

"So your sense of smell is sharper than normal?" said Jimmu.

"No," Goro said. "It's the same as yours, but I've learned how to use it better."

The meal was rice, stewed with vegetables and dried fish. It was the best food that Jimmu had eaten since leaving Mitsukage. "Thank you," he said to Yuki. "That was delicious."

"It was better than delicious!" said Ryu. "You're an excellent cook, Yuki."

"She wasn't always," Ichiro said. "Remember when we were first married, Yuki? Everything you cooked was raw, or burned."

"You ate it anyway," Yuki said with a smile.

"It was either eat, or starve!" said Ichiro.

Jimmu realized that Ichiro was playing a kind of game. By sharing a memory with Yuki, Ichiro was reminding Ryu of whose wife she was.

Ryu stood up, and brushed pine needles off his breeches. "I have to answer a call of nature," he said. "Jimmu, the horses could do with a drink. Will you fill their water bags?"

Jimmu nodded, and Ryu walked off between the trees.

"Ren will show you where to find water, Jimmu," said Goro.

Ren stiffened slightly.

"There's no need to bother Ren," Jimmu said.

"Ren doesn't mind," said Goro. He yawned. "It's time for my nap. I'll sleep in the wagon, and I don't want to be disturbed. I'll wake when I'm ready. While I'm asleep, I'll consider your proposition."

He's like a great lord, reflected Jimmu. He acts as if everything depends on him, and no one questions his orders. All the other blind men I've met were beggars.

Jimmu was not sure if he liked Goro, but he was beginning to admire him.

Ren led Jimmu to a pool that lay at the foot of a pile of boulders. The pool was fed by a spring that rose between the boulders, and fanned water over them. Jimmu hunkered down, and dipped the water bags into the pool.

As he drew the first bag from the water, Jimmu became aware that Ren was staring at him. "What's the matter?" Jimmu asked. "Haven't you seen a samurai fill a water bag before?"

Ren shrugged. "Nothing's the matter. I was just wondering about you."

"Oh?" said Jimmu. "And what were you wondering?"

Ren took this as an invitation to talk, and squatted at Jimmu's side. "Did you really kill ten bandits single-handed on your way to Mitsukage Castle?" he said.

"I don't remember," replied Jimmu.

"Have you killed many men?"

"I haven't kept count," Jimmu said.

"I've killed five!" announced Ren.

Jimmu took the second bag from the pool. "A true samurai doesn't boast about his exploits," he said. "His reputation should speak for itself."

"Samurai don't like us ninja, do they?" said Ren. "You must hate having to ask us for help."

"I'm doing it for Lady Takeko," Jimmu said.

Ren reached out his right hand and dabbled his fingers in the pool, sending ripples across the surface. "Is Lady Takeko as pretty as they say?"

Jimmu grunted. "That would depend on what they say, but yes, she's pretty."

"Are you in love with her?"

Jimmu had been asking himself the same thing, and he was careful with his answer. "As far as I know, I'm not in love with anyone."

"Does she love you?"

Jimmu found Ren's probing mildly irritating. "You shouldn't believe the gossip you've heard about me!" he warned. "Gossips exaggerate because it makes for a more interesting story, and foolish people believe the stories are true!"

A look of dismay came into Ren's eyes. "I didn't mean—" he said.

"I'm not offended," Jimmu said. "I was trying to explain that being in Lord Ankan's service means that it's my duty to protect him and his family."

"Even if it means risking your life?" said Ren.

"Certainly!" Jimmu said. "A samurai must be willing to sacrifice himself for his master."

Ren shook his head. "I don't want to be anybody's servant," he said. "I'd rather be free, and live life for myself."

Jimmu did not agree, but he kept his objections to himself. He put his hand on Ren's shoulder, and gave it a gentle squeeze. "We should be getting back," he said. "The others will be starting to think we're lost."

Ren moved his shoulder away from Jimmu's hand. His face was deeply flushed.

At dusk, Jimmu, Ryu, Ichiro, Yuki and Ren gathered around the embers of the fire, and ate leftover stew. As they were eating, Goro emerged from the wagon, and came to join them. Everyone watched expectantly as Goro sat down. "I've made a decision," he announced. "We will offer our assistance to Jimmu. Ryu has offered to pay our fee, but that won't be necessary. Once Lady Takeko is free, we will negotiate with her father for payment."

"You mean you'll hold her to ransom?" said Jimmu.

"I prefer to think that Lord Ankan will wish to reward us," Goro said. "The payment of our fee will show the other lords that he had no hand in his daughter's rescue, and his honour will stay intact."

Jimmu was relieved. "How many of your men will join us?" he said.

Goro frowned. "None," he said. "The six of us will be sufficient. After Ryu has described the layout of Tokoro Castle, I'll make a plan of attack."

"I've already made a plan," said Ryu. "We won't need to attack the castle. Lord Sabura will invite us inside."

"Why should he do that?" Goro said.

"Because a part of him has never grown up," said Ryu. "He delights in childish things. He loves to watch tumblers, conjurors – and puppet shows. All we have to do is turn up at Tokoro, and offer to put on a performance. Afterwards, when everyone is asleep, we can rescue Lady Takeko, and escape across the moat."

"That would mean abandoning the wagon and the oxen!" Yuki protested.

"Not necessarily," said Ryu. "We could hide the wagon in the woods near the castle, and go on foot from there."

"But surely someone in the castle will recognize you," Jimmu said.

"Once I've shaved off my hair, beard and moustache,

I doubt if I'll be able to recognize myself," said Ryu, "but I'll keep my face covered, and fake a limp."

Goro nodded. "What's your opinion of Ryu's plan, Ichiro?" he said.

"I don't like it," replied Ichiro. "It's too slick. Lord Sabura's weakness for puppet shows strikes me as a little too convenient. I smell a trap. It's true that Ryu is out for revenge, but not on Lord Sabura." He looked at Ryu. "You're after me, aren't you, Ryu? You still resent it that Yuki chose me over you."

Ryu's face turned pale; he rose to his feet. "Draw your sword, Ichiro!" he snarled. "You walked away from a fight with me once, but I won't let you walk away this time!"

Ichiro stood up. "Whenever you're ready, Ryu," he said.

Jimmu could hardly believe what was happening. He got up, and placed himself between Ichiro and Ryu. "Stop this!" he shouted. "What are you both thinking of? If you two want to fight, do it after Lady Takeko is safe!"

Ryu hung his head.

"I'm sorry!" he said hoarsely. "I lost control of

myself. It's only natural that Ichiro should be suspicious of me. I beg you all to forgive me."

He turned away, and walked off into the gathering darkness.

"I still don't trust him!" muttered Ichiro.

"Let's all sit down and talk calmly!" Goro said. "Ryu's plan seems sound enough — though of course, we'll have to make preparations."

"How long will that take?" asked Jimmu.

"That partly depends on you," Goro said. "You must learn a lot in a short time, and you'll begin tomorrow. Ren will teach you."

Jimmu thought that Goro was joking, and laughed. "What can Ren teach me?"

"How to be a puppeteer," said Goro.

When Ryu returned to the campfire, he was subdued and hardly spoke; but later, when he and Jimmu were settling down on their sleeping mats, he made his feelings clear. "You were right to talk to me the way you did, Jimmu," he said. "I'm embarrassed by my behaviour."

"Forget it, Ryu!" said Jimmu. "I did things in the past that I'm deeply ashamed of. It doesn't do to dwell on them."

"Agreed!" Ryu said. "So, you met your first ninja today. What d'you think of them?"

"Goro likes to play the cunning old man," said Jimmu. "Yuki is more of a listener than a talker, but I don't think much gets past her. I'd rather have Ichiro on my side than against me. The biggest puzzle is Ren. One minute he's bragging, the next he's almost in tears because he's annoyed me. He's the most peculiar boy I've ever met."

Ryu giggled.

"*The cat's fur is soft*
 But his teeth and claws are sharp.
He purrs – then pounces," he said.

"What does that mean?" said Jimmu.

"It means you've been taken in by outward appearances," Ryu said. "Ren may wear a boy's clothes, but she's obviously a girl!"

Jimmu felt a complete fool.

It had been the longest night Takeko had ever known. Too excited to sleep properly, she had lain awake for hours, thinking of all the things that could go wrong with her escape attempt. Eventually, to distract herself, she thought about Jimmu.

He had spent two years travelling to different places, and meeting different people; the experience was bound to have altered him. She had stayed at Mitsukage with her father; the only new acquaintance she had made was Hiki Sabura, and that had turned out to be a disaster.

I was a naive little fool! Takeko told herself, and it was true. She was the daughter of a provincial lord: her role in life was to make herself attractive to a potential suitor, marry him, and then become an obedient wife, and bear her husband's children so that he could continue his family line.

Lord Sabura had called her a rebel, and hinted that her involvement with Jimmu was a way of defying the conventions that bound her. Could he have been right? Had she been genuinely in love with Jimmu, or simply in love with the idea of being in love?

How can I know for sure? Takeko wondered.

Before she could find an answer, she heard a knock at the door, followed by Aki's voice. "Are you awake, My Lady?"

Takeko sat up, startled; she had been so deep in thought that she had not noticed the morning light shining around the edges of the closed shutters in her room. "Come in, Aki!" she called.

As soon as Aki was inside the room, she and Takeko moved quickly. Aki removed her clothes, and Takeko put them on. The last item of clothing was Aki's hat. Takeko placed it on her head, drew down the veil, and picked up the straw basket that Aki had brought with her. "Well?" she said.

"You'll do, My Lady," said Aki. "Lower your shoulders a bit more, and be sure to take small steps. If anyone questions you, tell them you're going to nurse your sick mother. Her name's Hina. She lives in the village of Danimura."

"Hina, in Danimura," Takeko repeated. "I'll remember." She embraced Aki. "Thank you for all that you've done," she said.

"Good luck, My Lady!" said Aki.

Takeko bound Aki's wrists and ankles with kimono sashes, gagged her with a silk scarf and, after murmuring an apology, scraped her fingernails across the maid's left cheek. Breathing deeply to calm herself, Takeko slid the door aside, went into the corridor, and turned left, passing the two soldiers who had stood guard through the night.

I'm Aki, she said to herself. I'm on my way to Danimura to nurse my mother, Hina.

She reached the stairs at the end of the corridor, and was about to go down them, when she heard footsteps behind her.

"Wait!" a voice said.

Takeko's heart thumped like a drum. She turned her head, and saw that one of the guards had left his post to follow her. "What is it?" she said, carefully mimicking Aki's accent. "What d'you want?"

The guard was young, and almost handsome. "I wanted to ask you something," he said.

Takeko was puzzled: the guard was not behaving like a man who was about to seize her and force her back to her room; he seemed bashful.

"I've had my eye on you for a while, Aki," he said. "I thought that maybe you'd like to..." His nerve failed him.

"Yes?" prompted Takeko, looking down so as to keep her face hidden.

The guard took a deep breath. "Step out with me!" he blurted. "Take some time for us to get to know each other better."

Relief made Takeko want to giggle, but she stopped herself. "What's your name, guardsman?" she asked.

"Daiki."

"Well, Daiki, I'll think about your offer," said Takeko. "Now you'd better get back to your post before an officer notices you're missing."

The guard turned smartly, and marched back along the corridor.

Takeko heaved a quiet sigh of relief that she had not been found out, and descended the stairs. When she reached the bottom, she opened the door facing her, and walked out into the courtyard.

The castle was preparing itself for the coming day. A groom was mucking out the stables, raking up the straw and horse dung into a heap. A line of men, stripped to their loincloths, chatted and joked as they waited to take their turn in the bathhouse.

Takeko crossed the courtyard, and stood by the main gate.

The daily ritual of the changing of the guard was taking place. It involved a lot of saluting and bowing. When the ritual ended, a shout went up: "Lower the drawbridge! Open the gate!"

Chains rattled; hinges creaked; the gate swung back.

Through the square arch of the gateway, Takeko saw wooded hills, their tops lit by the first rays of the sun; the valleys between them were still deep in shadow.

She stepped forwards.

Jimmu woke well before dawn. For a few minutes he tried to get back to sleep, but was unable to.

His mind took him back to the monastery at Okamori, and he heard Naoki's voice. "Why are you lying there wasting time, Jimmu? You've neglected your exercises. How can you expect to improve if you don't practise? You know that you'll never be perfect, but don't let that knowledge keep you from striving for perfection."

Jimmu sat up. The memory of Naoki had been his conscience talking to him. He had concentrated solely on the search for Goro, as if that were the end of his task. In fact, it was only the beginning, and to reach the end he had to be physically and mentally fit. Moving quietly, so as not to disturb Ryu, Jimmu rose from his blanket, grabbed his sword, and set off deeper into the wood.

Insects whined and buzzed in the darkness. Huge moths droned over his head; an owl screeched. Jimmu paid no attention. He was focused on himself, on his breathing, on the feel of the earth beneath his feet; he ignored the brambles that scratched his arms, and the grit that worked its way between his toes.

He halted at the pool Ren had shown him. He put down his sword, stripped off his top, and splashed water over his face, chest and back. The cold water shocked him, and a shivering fit set his teeth chattering. Jimmu doused himself with more and more water, until the shivering stopped.

He drew his sword from its sheath, and stood motionless. Both his hands were wrapped around the hilt of the sword. He was waiting for the perfect moment, and all at once he felt it rise in him, like a surfacing cormorant.

Jimmu brought the sword down from left to right, then shifted his grip, rolled his wrists, and brought the sword up in the opposite direction. He thrust and feinted, span around to parry imaginary blows from behind, jumping and ducking.

Time went away. Jimmu was unaware of the sky changing from black to grey, and he did not hear the birds singing as the rim of the sun showed above the horizon. He continued with his exercises, and the drops of water on his body were gradually replaced with drops of sweat.

Jimmu's muscles told him when they had done enough. He came to a standstill in the same pose in which he had begun: feet apart, both hands gripping his sword.

"That was impressive!" someone said.

Jimmu wheeled to his right.

Ren was seated on an upturned pail. Her elbows were propped on her knees; her chin was resting on the palms of her hands. She wore her hair loose, and it hung down, framing her face and concealing her protruding ears. At that moment, nobody would have mistaken her for a boy.

"How long have you been there?" said Jimmu.

"Long enough to see how good you are," said Ren. "When you switched the sword from your right hand to your left just now, it was like the sword hung in the air, waiting for you. How did you do that?"

Jimmu slotted the sword back into its scabbard. "Why didn't you tell me you were a girl yesterday?" he said.

"I didn't think you needed to be told," said Ren.

"And what was all that nonsense about killing five men?" Jimmu said. "Girls can't fight – they don't know how!"

Ren stood, raised her hands above her head, and launched herself into a double cartwheel. Jimmu instinctively stepped back to avoid colliding with her, and as she passed him, Ren landed a kick to his stomach that winded him, and he doubled over.

"Well?" said Ren, as Jimmu straightened himself. "D'you still think that girls can't fight?"

"That wasn't fair!" protested Jimmu. "I wasn't ready for you!"

He lunged towards Ren. She swerved away, moved behind Jimmu, and kicked his backside.

Jimmu leaped on Ren, and caught hold of her tunic, intending to wrestle her to the ground.

Ren rolled backwards and, using his own weight against him, threw Jimmu into the pool.

The icy water took Jimmu's breath away. He clambered out of the pool, and bowed to Ren. "I'm sorry," he said. "I behaved arrogantly, and I apologize. You've proved that girls can fight, or at least that *you* can fight."

Ren burst out laughing. "I'm sorry, Jimmu," she gasped, "but you're so – wet!"

Jimmu glanced down at his dripping clothes.

"You look ridiculous!" hooted Ren.

"It's no more than I deserve," Jimmu said, and he joined in with Ren's laughter.

*

When Jimmu and Ren returned to the others, no one commented on the state of Jimmu's clothes. Everyone was occupied. Yuki was kneading dough in a wooden bowl. Ryu was on his hands and knees, coaxing a flame from a bundle of kindling. Goro and Ichiro were by the wagon, talking with their heads close together.

"Are we going to break camp, Goro?" Jimmu called out.

"Why?" asked Goro.

Jimmu frowned. "I thought we might be starting out for Tokoro Castle today," he said.

"We're not ready yet, Jimmu," said Goro. "I told you, there are preparations to make."

Jimmu groaned in exasperation.

"You must be patient, Jimmu," said Goro. "Has Ren given you a puppetry lesson yet?"

"I thought you were joking about that," Jimmu said.

"It was no joke," Goro assured him. "Putting on puppet shows is an excellent disguise. We can travel anywhere without arousing suspicion, but we must be entertaining. The better the show, the more effective the disguise."

"And puppeteering is good training for a ninja," added Ichiro. "Most of our performances are at night, in the courtyards of inns, or a suitable spot in a village. I'm sure you've seen puppeteers in action, Jimmu, in their black robes, their faces hidden, creeping about the stage behind their puppets. When a show goes well, the audience stop noticing the puppeteers, they only see the puppets, acting out the story that Goro tells. Puppeteering takes great skill."

"But do I have time to learn?" asked Jimmu. "In twenty days from now, Lord Ankan will send reinforcements to Lord Nobunaga, and Lady Takeko will be put to death."

"Then you'd better work hard, and learn fast," Goro advised. "Lady Takeko's life depends on our success."

After the morning meal, Jimmu helped Ren to unload a chest from the wagon. Ren opened the chest, and took out the stick puppet of a young noblewoman, dressed in a miniature silk kimono, richly embroidered. The puppet was half life-sized; its head and hands had been skilfully carved from wood, and stained with dye.

"Isn't she beautiful?" said Ren. "She's Princess Kayuga. In our show, Goro tells the story of how she was wooed by five foolish suitors, while Ichiro plays the flute to set the mood. I work the princess. Yuki and I share the rest of the puppets between us. That can be complicated, so having another puppeteer will help things to run more smoothly."

Jimmu was not in a positive mood. "I doubt that I'll be any help," he said. "A samurai doesn't play with children's toys!"

"They're not toys!" Ren insisted.

"What are they then?" asked Jimmu.

"I'll show you," said Ren.

She began to work the puppet. The princess put her hands together, lifted them to her face, and bowed to Jimmu. The movements were so lifelike that Jimmu automatically returned the bow.

Ren laughed. "Do you always bow to children's toys, Samurai?"

"I couldn't help it!" confessed Jimmu. "Just for a moment, I thought that she was real."

"That's because *I* believe that she's real," Ren said. "If you aren't convinced that the puppets are alive, the audience won't be convinced either, and they won't enjoy the show." She put down the princess, and selected another puppet from the chest: a plump nobleman, with an upturned nose and a ridiculously tall hat. "This is Prince Kurumamochi," she said. "He's vain and sly. He tries to win the princess by cheating. I think you'd make a fine Prince Kurumamochi."

Jimmu ignored Ren's insult. "Have you got to teach

me here, in front of everybody?" he asked quietly. "Can't we go somewhere quiet?"

Ren relished Jimmu's embarrassment. "What's the matter, Jimmu? Are you afraid of being laughed at?" she mocked; then she relented. "All right. There's a clearing not far away. We'll go there."

Jimmu's introduction to the art of puppetry did not go well. He mixed up the sticks that controlled the arms with the stick that moved the head, and once he fumbled so badly that he almost dropped the puppet.

Ren was not a patient teacher. Though she found Jimmu's mistakes funny at first, it was not long before she became irritated with him. "You're so clumsy!" she chided. "I can't believe you're the same person I saw exercising earlier. If you can handle a sword, you can work a puppet. Concentrate! Forget that you're a samurai, and turn yourself into a prince!"

That was the moment that Jimmu stopped worrying about looking foolish, and started trying to prove to Ren that he could master this new skill. He held the puppet upright, and thought of all the arrogant nobles he had met. He manipulated the puppet carefully, imitating the gait of the imperial courtiers he had seen in Kyoto.

"Much better!" exclaimed Ren.

The puppet turned its head, and peered down its nose at her. "In polite society, it is considered vulgar for a young lady to raise her voice," Jimmu made it say.

Ren was delighted. "Now you're starting to understand!" she declared.

They played a scene together. Princess Kayuga was radiant, but modest. Prince Kurumamochi paraded around her, puffed up with self-importance. Jimmu and Ren repeated the scene over and over again, until their arms ached so badly that they were forced to take a rest.

Ren used her sleeve to wipe the sweat from her forehead. "You know what, Jimmu?" she said. "If we keep at it, you might make a half-decent puppeteer."

Jimmu was surprised by how much pleasure Ren's compliment gave him.

*

When Jimmu and Ren returned to camp at midday, Goro was sitting with his back against the wagon. He had put on a straw hat, and was quietly snoring in its shade. Yuki was on the opposite side of the camp, sharpening a sword on a stone. Jimmu and Ren went over to her.

"Where are Ryu and Ichiro?" asked Jimmu.

"Ichiro is getting some equipment ready," said Yuki. "Goro sent Ryu to the nearest farmhouse to buy fresh food. I think Ryu was glad of the chance to be on his own for a time."

Jimmu frowned: he thought that Ryu would have done better to stay in camp, and try to make up for his outburst the previous evening.

"Will you fetch water for the oxen, Ren?" asked Yuki.

Ren nodded. "Coming, Jimmu?"

Yuki set aside the sword, and took a length of twine from the sash around her waist. "Jimmu is staying with me," she said. "I have to measure him."

"Why?" said Jimmu.

"Because you and Ryu must be fitted with ninja outfits," Yuki said. "They're the same kind of clothes puppeteers wear, completely black, with a scarf covering all our faces except our eyes. It helps the audience to concentrate on the puppets."

Ren picked up a pail, and went off in the direction of the pool.

Yuki stretched the twine across the back of Jimmu's shoulders. "Hold your arms out straight," she instructed him.

"That's a fine sword you were sharpening," said Jimmu. "Whose is it?"

"Mine," Yuki said. "I took it from a drunken samurai."

"What happened?" asked Jimmu.

"I broke his spine," Yuki replied. "Turn round, so I can measure your chest."

Jimmu's heart beat faster; there was a steeliness about Yuki that made him wary. "Are all ninja women fighters?" he asked.

"When they have to be," Yuki replied. She stepped back, and looked directly into Jimmu's eyes. "Be careful with Ren."

"Careful?"

"She doesn't have much experience of young men,"

Yuki said. "Because of the stories she's heard about you, she thinks you're a hero. Don't take advantage of her."

Jimmu took offence. "Are you threatening me?" he said.

"I'm offering advice," said Yuki. "We'll be fighting together as a team. Personal feelings mustn't affect our judgement."

"Then I give you my word that I'll be no more to her than a friend," Jimmu said.

Goro stirred, and woke. "Is that you, Jimmu?" he called. "Are you a puppeteer yet?"

"Not yet, Goro, but I'm on my way to becoming one," said Jimmu.

Two guards at the main gate of Tokoro Castle stood in front of Takeko to bar her way. One of them placed his hand on her left shoulder. "You're not thinking of leaving, are you, Takeko?" he said.

Takeko yelped in horror as she realized that the guard was Lord Sabura in disguise; she had been so intent on her escape that she had failed to recognize him. She shrugged herself free from his grasp, and began to cry.

"You seem a little disappointed, Takeko!" Lord Sabura said.

"You tricked me!" sobbed Takeko.

"To be strictly accurate, Aki is the one who tricked you, though I must admit that I coached her," Lord Sabura said. "Did you like the story of the bird catcher? Entirely my own invention. I imagine Aki told it movingly though."

Takeko's hopes collapsed into despair: there was no escaping from the castle or Lord Sabura; she would never see her home, her father, or Jimmu, again. "Why don't you just hand me over to your torturer and have done with it?" said Takeko.

Lord Sabura sighed. "People's reactions to physical torment are too predictable!" he said. "They shriek, and shout, and writhe around, and beg you to stop. There is no artistry in that kind of torture. It takes a subtle intellect to inflict mental discomfort, and the wounds it causes take longer to heal."

He reached out to Takeko, and she shrank away.

"I only want to remove your hat, Takeko!" Lord

Sabura explained. "You should not cover your beauty beneath a veil."

Takeko ripped off the hat, and flung it to the ground; she glared at Lord Sabura. "There!" she said. "You don't care about my beauty – it's my tears you want to see, isn't it?"

"Ah, dear Takeko, your stubbornness is one of your most attractive qualities!" purred Lord Sabura. "Without it, playing games with you would be nowhere near as satisfying. I am seriously considering a revision of my plans for you."

"D'you expect me to care?" Takeko snorted.

"I thought that you might take an interest, since it concerns your life," said Lord Sabura. "It might suit me better to spare you, and make you my wife. I expect Takeda Katsuyori to defeat Oda Nobunaga, but if he does not, it may prove beneficial to me to be married to the daughter of one of Lord Nobunaga's most trusted allies."

"I'd rather die!" Takeko hissed.

And it struck her that she had stumbled upon the best exit from her situation. If she killed herself, her father could go into battle with a clear conscience, and Lord Sabura would no longer be able to taunt her.

Takeko decided that, as soon as she had the means and the opportunity, she would take her own life in the time-honoured way.

Chapter 12
10TH DAY, 5TH MONTH, 1575

When Yuki had finished taking Jimmu's measurements, Goro beckoned him over to the wagon.

"I'm going for a walk, Jimmu," Goro said. "Would you care to keep me company?"

"Of course," said Jimmu. He helped the old man to his feet, and they set off between the trees.

"I was intrigued by what you told me yesterday about Lord Nobunaga," Goro said. "Lord Ankan is one of his most faithful allies. It's curious that Lord Nobunaga will not allow him to attempt Lady Takeko's rescue."

It was clear to Jimmu that Goro was fishing for information, and his reply was meant to be dismissive. "Who knows what goes through the minds of great lords?"

"Someone who pays attention to details," Goro

said. "Lord Nobunaga has laid in a large supply of gunpowder in his capital at Gifu. The gunsmiths of Owari Province have been busy for weeks, working late into the night to meet His Lordship's order for muskets. Lord Katsuyori has boasted that he'll destroy Lord Nobunaga, but I have an inkling that the Takeda will get an unpleasant surprise before the campaign season is over."

They walked to the edge of the wood, almost as far as the road to Izumison. Goro sat down on a thick bed of moss, and rested his staff against his right shoulder. "You get on well with Ren," he said.

"What makes you think that?" said Jimmu.

"When you came back from your puppetry lesson, the two of you walked in step," Goro said.

Jimmu became defensive. "I'm not sure whether we get on or not," he said. "She's an...unusual girl."

"In some ways, but not in others," said Goro. "Yuki was right to warn you."

Jimmu frowned. "I thought you were asleep when Yuki said that."

"I pretended," Goro admitted. "Most old men think they're cunning, and in my case, it happens to be true."

"So why did you bring me here, cunning old man?" said Jimmu.

"To tutor you," Goro said. "I leave puppetry to Ren. I'm going to teach you how to think like a ninja."

"Don't all warriors think alike?" Jimmu wondered aloud. "They aim to use their skills to overcome their opponents."

"But they go about it in different ways," Goro said. "In battle, a samurai wears a crest on his helmet so that he can be identified, and before he challenges an opponent to single combat, he recites a list of the warriors he has defeated. A ninja must move silently, and be as weightless and invisible as a shadow in the dark."

Goro's words provoked troubling memories in Jimmu. "I know how to be stealthy," he said. "The samurai who raised me trained me as an assassin."

"Araki Nichiren!" murmured Goro.

Jimmu could not conceal his astonishment. "Is there *anything* about me that you don't know, Goro?" he exclaimed.

"I know more about you than you know about

yourself, Shimomura Jimmu," said Goro. "I pieced your story together from talk I heard as I travelled with the puppet troupe. Gathering information is vital to the ninja way of life."

It had been so long since anyone had called Jimmu by his full name that it sounded strange to him. He shook his head. "There's no such person as Shimomura Jimmu, Goro. After my father's treachery, the Emperor issued a proclamation that ended the existence of the Shimomura Clan."

"The name still exists inside you, Jimmu," said Goro. "You can't deny what's in your blood, and you can't escape from it either. Perhaps it's your destiny to restore your family's honour."

"It's my destiny to be Lord Ankan's samurai," Jimmu insisted. "He has offered to adopt me into the Choju Clan. When he does, I'll have a name I can be proud of."

"Maybe so," said Goro. He used his staff to lever himself upright. "Show me how stealthy you are. See if you can take my staff off me. I won't try and stop you, unless I hear you."

"I'm too old to play games!" Jimmu said, thinking

that there was no skill involved in stealing from a blind man.

"Humour me," insisted Goro. "It won't be as straightforward as you think."

Jimmu walked some distance away from Goro, and circled him, to make an approach from behind. He moved cautiously, avoiding the branches of shrubs so that their rustling leaves would not give him away.

I'm as light as a snowflake, he told himself. I'm as silent as a spider spinning its web.

Jimmu paused before he took his first step onto the bed of moss. Goro showed no sign that he was aware of how close Jimmu was.

It would be easy to jump the rest of the way, and snatch the staff, Jimmu thought, but it would be sweeter to creep up on Goro, and take him by surprise.

The moss was soft and springy; Jimmu felt as if he were walking on silk. He inched forwards until Goro was almost within his reach.

With the suppleness of a cat, Goro twisted from the waist, and brought the tip of his staff down on Jimmu's right shin.

Jimmu gasped in pain.

"A good effort!" said Goro. "However, you'll have to do better if you're going to catch me out."

Jimmu crouched down to rub his throbbing leg. "*Can* you be caught out, Goro?" he said.

"Only with great difficulty," said Goro. "Without the difficulty, there would be no fun."

"You have a strange sense of fun, Goro," Jimmu said.

"So I've often been told," said Goro. "Now try to take my staff again, and if you succeed, I'll give you a reward."

"What reward?" asked Jimmu.

"The pleasure of not being hit," Goro said.

Lord Sabura had changed out of his guard's disguise, and was wearing a kimono with a pattern of white ginkgo leaves on a dark green background. He sat in his private chamber, staring at a black koi carp swimming in a porcelain bowl. The fish's billowing fins and tail were edged with orange.

Takeko was kneeling opposite Lord Sabura,

watching him watch the fish. Behind her, the chief maid of Tokoro Castle sat with her head respectfully lowered.

"This fish swims round and round without ceasing," Lord Sabura said abruptly. "It is almost as if it were searching for a way out. Do you think that it knows it is trapped, Takeko?"

Takeko knew that he was trying to provoke her by drawing a comparison between herself and the koi, but she was too numb with misery to react. "I've no way of telling, Sabura," she replied.

"You were highly distressed this morning, but you seem to have made a remarkably fast recovery, Takeko," observed Lord Sabura. "You appear to be resigned to your situation, yet I sense that you are keeping something hidden. Could it be that you have decided to do something drastic?"

"I don't know what you mean, Sabura," Takeko said.

Lord Sabura looked straight into Takeko's eyes. "You know very well what I mean," he said. "Chief maid! See to it that all sharp objects, such as hairpins and metal combs, are taken from Lady Takeko. Her room is to be stripped of any sashes or cords that she might use to hang herself. The shutters in her room will be nailed shut. A maid must stay with her at all times so that she is never left alone. Should Lady Takeko do herself any injury, I shall hold you personally responsible — is that clear?"

The chief maid bowed low. "I will make the necessary arrangements, My Lord," she said.

Chapter 13
11TH – 17TH DAY, 5TH MONTH, 1575

For the next few days, Jimmu trained as a ninja; it was a period of intense activity. Yuki instructed him in unarmed combat, teaching him new holds, and throws that added to the bruises he had received from Ren and Goro. Jimmu also learned how to use his hands as weapons, delivering blows that could kill, or render an opponent unconscious.

Ichiro trained Jimmu in the handling of ninja weapons. At their first session, he showed Jimmu a small sickle attached to a length of chain.

"This is a shinobi-gama," Ichiro explained. "If you sweep the chain sideways, it wraps itself around your enemy's ankles, so you can pull him down, and finish him off with the blade. It's most useful in the dark, in places where there isn't room to swing a sword."

"But that's a cowardly way to fight!" blurted Jimmu.

Ichiro gave Jimmu a hard stare. "There's something you have to understand, Jimmu," he said. "Ninja don't fight for honour or glory. All that matters is the outcome of the mission — in this case, freeing Lady Takeko. If that means taking a guard by surprise and stabbing him in the back, it has to be done without hesitation. Among ninja there are no heroes or cowards, only successes or failures."

"I'd still rather use a sword," muttered Jimmu.

Ichiro shook his head at Jimmu's stubbornness. "All right," he said. "Since you don't approve of the shinobi-gama, let's see how you take to this."

Ichiro reached into the left sleeve of his jerkin, and drew out a flat metal disc with seven spikes running around its outer edge. "This is a throwing star," he informed Jimmu. "At close range it's as good as a bow, but it's quieter, and easier to carry. Using it effectively takes a great deal of skill."

Jimmu thought that Ichiro was challenging him. "Let me try!" he said eagerly.

Ichiro passed over the throwing star.

"What shall I aim for?" asked Jimmu.

Ichiro pointed. "That tree over there," he said.

"See if you can hit it at about neck height."

Jimmu raised the star.

"Wait, you're not holding it properly!" said Ichiro.

Jimmu ignored Ichiro's warning, and hurled the star as hard as he could. It tumbled wildly through the air before landing on the ground, well short of its target.

Ichiro went to retrieve the star, and carried it back to Jimmu. "You have to hold the star so that it slants to one side," he said. "As you throw it, give it a flick with your wrist." A thought occurred to Ichiro, and he smiled at it. "Did you ever play at skimming stones across a pond when you were a boy?"

"When I was a boy, I was taught how to be a samurai," Jimmu said. "I wasn't allowed to play."

"Then it's time you did," said Ichiro. "Let's go to the pool. We'll pick up some stones along the way."

By the end of the session, Jimmu's throwing arm was sore, but he could skim a stone across the pool, and make a throwing star go in more or less the direction he wanted. He was fascinated by the weapon, and became determined to master it. He took to carrying a throwing star with him so that he could practise whenever he had a spare moment; as a result, he made steady progress.

Through the training sessions, Jimmu came to know Yuki and Ichiro a little better. Although Yuki was quiet and reserved, when something amused her, she laughed infectiously. Ichiro was a considerate teacher, giving Jimmu more praise than criticism. Jimmu admired Ichiro's inner strength, and the graceful ease with which he moved.

As well as unarmed combat and weaponry, Jimmu was drilled in how to climb with iron claws fitted to his hands and feet, how to scale a ladder made from silk cord and bamboo, and in some basic escape techniques.

He began to see the truth behind some of the legends about ninja making themselves invisible, and scaling sheer walls as easily as a fly.

Jimmu enjoyed his training, but he was constantly aware that time was passing as rapidly as a river swollen by heavy rain. The day set for Takeko's execution was drawing closer, and it made him push himself even harder.

*

Ren wanted Jimmu to try out more characters in the story of Princess Kayuga, so one overcast morning they carried the chest of puppets to the clearing. Jimmu started by playing Prince Kurumamochi again, and this time it came easily to him. His hands knew how to work the puppet so that it gestured smoothly. Ren joined in with the puppet of Princess Kayuga, and they acted out a little scene.

"You did that well!" said Ren.

"I didn't do anything," Jimmu said. "I let the prince do as he wanted."

Ren smiled; Jimmu returned the smile, without worrying about Yuki's disapproval.

"I like it when you smile," said Ren. "It makes you look different."

"In a good way, or a bad way?" Jimmu said.

"Most of the time you look serious, like you're in a bad mood," said Ren, "but when you smile, it's as if you're somebody else. I can see what you looked like when you were a child, and what you'll look like when you're an old man."

A gust of wind blew a strand of hair across Ren's face, and as she reached up to push the strand back into place, something struck Jimmu.

She's as beautiful as the princess, he thought. When we first met I thought she was a boy, and now she's a beautiful girl. How did she transform herself?

"Try another puppet!" urged Ren. "One of the foolish suitors is a chief minister – see what you can do with him."

The chief minister was thin, with an elaborate topknot. Jimmu based the character's movements on a customs official he had known in Nagasaki, a fussy man who bustled everywhere.

Ren laughed until tears came into her eyes. "That's perfect, Jimmu!" she said. "You make him so funny. What gave you the idea?"

Jimmu told her about the customs official, and suddenly he and Ren were deep in conversation. Jimmu talked about his warrior pilgrimage, and the year he had spent in the monastery at Okamori; he used the puppet to imitate Naoki's walk.

Ren described her childhood, and how much she had adored her father, a ninja. "When I was thirteen, he went on a mission and never came back," she said. "I went wild. I picked fights with other girls – and boys too. I stole things. My mother couldn't control me. She beat me. That went on for a year or more. Then came a morning when I woke up, and realized how wild I was. I hated the person I'd become. I knew I had to change, and find something to give my life meaning. So I went to Goro, and asked him to train me to be a ninja, like my father."

"Did he get you to try and take his staff away from him?" Jimmu asked.

"Yes – painful, isn't it?" said Ren.

They both laughed.

"What is it about you, Ren?" Jimmu said. "Girls usually make me uncomfortable, but I can relax when I'm with you."

Ren shrugged. "It's because we're both fighters," she said. "You think of me as an equal, and you forget that I'm a girl."

As she spoke, the sun came out from behind a cloud, and a ray of light shone on her face, making her look so lovely that Jimmu held his breath. He suddenly felt awkward, and covered it by pretending to cough. "You're right, Ren," he said. "I'd forgotten that you were a girl."

Jimmu and Ren returned to camp, and found the others gathered around the fire.

"You're just in time!" Goro greeted them. "Ryu is about to show us the layout of Tokoro Castle."

When Jimmu and Ren had taken their places, Ryu used a pointed stick to scratch a diagram on a patch of earth in front of the fire. "There are thick woods all around Tokoro," he said. "We'll leave the wagon, the oxen and the horses there, and go the rest of the way on foot. The castle is surrounded by a deep moat. During the day, a drawbridge connects the main gate to a causeway. At night, the drawbridge is raised. After performing for Lord Sabura, we'll bed down in the courtyard, and wait for things to go quiet. Then we'll enter through a door near the stables, and go up the staircase to the first floor."

Ryu scratched a second diagram, showing a row of squares joined by two parallel lines. "This is a plan of Lord Sabura's private apartments," he said. "The room next to them is reserved for honoured guests, and it's where Lady Takeko will be. Guards will be posted in the corridor."

"How many guards?" asked Ichiro.

"At least two, no more than four," Ryu said. "When they've been taken care of, Jimmu should go in to Lady Takeko's room," said Ryu. "After he's made himself known to her, we'll follow him, and escape through the shutters. We'll need ropes and hooks. Jimmu can help Lady Takeko to swim across the moat. Yuki and Ren will look after Goro. Ichiro and I will arrange a diversion. Any ideas, Ichiro?"

"If we set fire to the room, it should cause plenty of confusion and panic," Ichiro said.

Jimmu was sceptical. To his way of thinking, the only way to storm a castle was to lay siege to it, and attack in force. "I'm not convinced your plan will work, Ryu," he said. "It relies too heavily on surprise."

"You're wrong, Jimmu," said Goro. "It relies on our being certain of what we're doing, while keeping our opponents uncertain. If you're not confident about Ryu's plan, be confident about yourself, and you'll succeed."

"It's like puppetry, Jimmu," Ren said. "You have to believe."

That afternoon, Jimmu trained with Goro in their usual place, near the bed of moss. Jimmu still could not manage to get close enough to snatch Goro's staff, but he had learned how to dodge most of the blows that Goro aimed at him.

It was hot, and so humid that even Goro broke into a sweat. "Enough! I must rest," he announced.

Jimmu and Goro sat together on the edge of the moss bed. Goro wiped his forehead with his sleeve. "You've done well today, Jimmu," he said. "You're starting to think like a ninja."

Jimmu smiled. "If anyone had said that to me a few days ago, I would have taken it as an insult," he said.

"And now?" asked Goro.

"I'm beginning to understand that, in their own way, ninja are as dedicated as samurai," Jimmu said.

Just then, a breeze sprang up, carrying the sound of angry voices from the direction of the Izumison Road.

Goro cocked his head to one side. "Is that Ryu?" he murmured. "Who's he arguing with? Go and see if he needs help, Jimmu, but be sure and stay out of sight."

Jimmu kept low as he moved through the undergrowth, carefully avoiding any branches that might rustle, and dry twigs that might snap and give him away. When he reached the edge of the trees, he crouched down.

Ryu was at the side of the road, talking to a mounted soldier who wore the back flag of the Hiki Clan. As far as Jimmu could see, Ryu was unarmed.

"I've told you all I know!" Ryu said to the soldier. "Don't you trust my word?"

"Why should I trust you?" replied the soldier. "Everyone in Tokoro knows what a liar you are, Yasuda Ryu."

"But this time I swear it's the truth!" Ryu insisted.

Jimmu reached inside the fold of his top, and brought out his throwing star.

"Wait here with me!" the soldier ordered Ryu. "The others will be here soon. My commander will decide whether you're speaking the truth or not." His hand went down to the hilt of his sword.

Jimmu hurled the throwing star, but in his eagerness to use the weapon, he misjudged the height. Instead of striking the soldier's throat, the star glanced off the lacquered panels of the armour covering the man's left shoulder. The soldier immediately kicked his heels into the flanks of his horse, and galloped away.

Jimmu broke cover, and hurried to Ryu's side.

Ryu's eyes bulged furiously. "What did you do that for?" he raged. "I almost had him convinced that you and I went our separate ways three days ago!"

"I thought he was going to take you prisoner," said Jimmu.

"You should have let him!" Ryu snapped. "He's an advance scout for a search party. They know we left Izumison looking for a troupe of puppeteers. Their commander must have paid the landlady of the inn more than I did."

Jimmu frowned. "How did the scout manage to find you, Ryu?" he asked.

"Because I wasn't thinking clearly," said Ryu. "There's no time to explain. We must get back to camp and warn the others so that we can hide."

Goro stepped out of the trees. "There's no point in hiding," he said.

"How long have you been skulking there in the shadows, Goro?" said Ryu.

"Long enough to know we must let the search party find us," Goro said.

"Are you mad?" exclaimed Ryu.

"Far from it," said Goro. "Unlike you, my mind is working perfectly clearly, Ryu. If the soldiers return to Tokoro Castle and report what they have learned to Lord Sabura, he will be highly suspicious of any puppeteers who make an approach to him, and our element of surprise will be lost. The only way to save our mission is to let them find us, and kill them all."

Takeko and Lord Sabura were in the reception room at Tokoro. Lord Sabura was drinking green tea, and eating cakes that had been coloured and shaped to resemble leaves and flowers. Takeko sat motionless, with her hands in her lap; her head was lowered so that her unpinned hair hung over her face.

Lord Sabura munched, sipped, and swallowed. "Is it the bitterness of the tea that causes the cakes to taste sweeter, or does the sweetness of the cakes make the tea seem more bitter?" he mused aloud. "What do you think, Takeko?"

"I don't know, Sabura," Takeko replied.

Lord Sabura was irritated by the flat tone of her voice. "Your newfound meekness does not suit you, Takeko," he said. "I think that I preferred you when you were insolent."

"I'm sorry you don't approve, Sabura," said Takeko.

Lord Sabura wiped his mouth with a silk napkin. "I thought that you might be interested to learn the most recent information I have received concerning Jimmu," he said slyly.

Takeko made no response.

Lord Sabura's irritation increased: he had expected Takeko to gasp, or at least start. "He was last reported riding north, in the direction of Iga Province," he said. "So it seems he has decided not to be a doomed lover after all."

"It doesn't matter to me," said Takeko.

"If I were in your place, I would be angry with him," Lord Sabura said. "Not many young men are granted an opportunity to turn their lives into poetry. This Jimmu of yours may well be handsome and courageous, but he has no artistic insight. When he is not on the battlefield, he is no better than an animal."

"If you say so, Sabura," said Takeko.

"This is tiresome!" Lord Sabura snapped. "I advise you to alter your attitude, or—"

"Or you'll have me put to death?" said Takeko.

Lord Sabura's anger vanished in a laugh. "Ah, I see!" he exclaimed. "You hope to provoke me into ordering your execution, is that it?"

"Do as you please," said Takeko. "I don't care any more."

As soon as Jimmu, Goro and Ryu were back at the camp, Goro quickly outlined the situation to the others, and then issued precise instructions for the coming battle with the scouting party.

"Arm yourselves with bows," Goro said. "The soldiers know that we're expecting them, so they'll divide their attack. Some will charge at us head on, and try to pin us down, while the rest work their way round us."

"How can you be sure, Goro?" asked Jimmu.

"Because that's what I would do in their position," Goro said. "We must put green wood on the fire to make smoke that can be seen from the road so the search party will know where we are. Ichiro, hide in the bamboo in front of the wagon. Ryu, go into the trees at the far side of the fire. Yuki and I will be behind the wagon, and we'll pick off any soldiers who might get through. Jimmu, guard the track to the pool. If the enemy comes that way they'll be on foot, so keep your eyes and ears open. Ren, stay on Jimmu's left. Climb a tree so that you can shoot from above. Bear in mind that they'll try their hardest to distract us – don't let them. We work as a team. Each of us is expendable. If one falls, the rest must fight on. Now, make ready to receive our guests."

Jimmu took up position, ignoring the feeling of excitement that was building up inside him. He strung his bow, and stuck seven arrows into the earth so that they would be close to hand. His movements were slow and methodical. All the time he scanned the forest, and listened carefully for the chattering of startled birds that might give away the position of the enemy.

Jimmu's mind returned to the Izumison Road. What had Ryu been doing there, just as a Hiki scout happened by? Why had Ryu been unarmed? Was it bad luck, coincidence, or something more sinister?

The sound of drumming hoofs drove the questions from Jimmu's mind, and he looked back towards the camp. Five riders were approaching, their horses weaving between the trees. The riders squatted low in their saddles, but not low enough. Ichiro took one man down with a well-aimed arrow; Ryu killed another with an arrow that pierced the soldier's neck.

Three riders broke through into the camp clearing. Ren's arrow hit one man in the side, lifting him out of the saddle. His horse missed its footing, fell, and rolled over, crushing him. Ichiro put an arrow deep inside the second rider's chest. The third urged his horse to jump over the fire, and then wheeled round, intending to attack Ichiro.

Yuki emerged from behind the wagon, with a drawn sword. The blade flashed, and the rider fell.

A wave of five more mounted men advanced through the forest.

Jimmu jerked his head to his left when he heard Ren cry out. She had slipped off her branch, and was clinging on with both hands, kicking her legs to try and swing herself back onto it. The branches of the undergrowth around the tree twitched as three soldiers headed for her; they would be on her in seconds.

A shock of fear and dismay went through Jimmu. If he stayed where he was, Ren would die, and he could not allow that to happen. He left his post and raced towards the soldiers, drawing his sword, and yelling loudly to attract their attention.

The nearest soldier jabbed with his sword. Jimmu twisted aside, and felt the point of the sword rip through the right sleeve of his top. He countered with a vicious slash, arcing down from right to left, slicing his opponent open.

Time seemed to slow down. Jimmu faced the remaining two soldiers, who moved as clumsily as if they were underwater. One had his sword raised above his head. Jimmu struck low, and cut the man's legs off at the knees. The last soldier's nerve failed, and he ran away. Jimmu raced after him, and killed him with a blow to the back of the neck that severed the soldier's spine.

Jimmu's face was spattered with blood. He wiped the worst of it away before glancing up at Ren, who was clambering back onto the branch. "Are you all right?" he called out.

"Behind you!" screeched Ren.

Jimmu wheeled round. A dozen or more soldiers were charging down the track he was supposed to be guarding, fanning out into a straggling line. Jimmu's heart sank; he had failed the team. He raised his sword, and ran at the attackers.

The world shrank to a nightmare of grimacing faces and clashing weapons. Jimmu felt the jolt of his blade passing through the flesh and bone of one opponent, and then the next seemed to spring up out of the ground. His ears rang with the shrieks of the wounded, and the whinnying of horses. A pall of dust rose over the camp, stinging Jimmu's eyes, and filling his mouth with a bitter taste. He had no idea how many he killed, or how often he came near to death.

And suddenly it was over: he was swinging his sword at nothing, and blood was dripping from a gash on his right forearm.

The campsite was littered with bodies, some lying still, some trying to crawl along. Ryu had come out into the open. Ichiro stood with his arms wrapped around Yuki. Ren sat slumped at the edge of the clearing. Goro was standing by the cart.

A lone rider was cantering off towards the road, slapping his horse's rump.

"Don't let him get away!" shouted Goro.

Ichiro let go of Yuki, nocked an arrow onto his bow,

and trained it on a spot in front of the rider. He loosed the arrow in the same split second it took the horse and rider to cross a gap between two trees. The point of the arrow found the gap in the back plates of the soldier's armour, and he crashed to the ground.

Ryu drew his dagger, and began the grim business of slitting the throats of the wounded.

Jimmu walked slowly over to Goro, and hung his head in shame. "I let you down," he said.

"You let us all down, and you chose a bad time to do it," retorted Goro. "Why did you leave your position?"

"Ren was in danger," said Jimmu.

"And so you decided to put the whole mission at risk?" snorted Goro.

"I'm sorry," said Jimmu. "I forgot myself. It won't happen again."

But he knew that he was lying. He had gone to Ren's aid because he could not bear the thought of losing her, and it had made him realize that his feelings for her went far deeper than friendship.

Ryu strode across the clearing, cleaning his dagger with a piece of rag. "It's done," he said to Goro. "They're all dead – no thanks to you, Jimmu."

"Jimmu made an error of judgement, and afterwards fought bravely to redeem himself," said Goro. "But what about you, Ryu? What were you doing on the Izumison Road earlier?"

Ryu shrugged. "I went for a walk to clear my head," he said. "I didn't know where I was until the Hiki scout rode along. He recognized me and stopped. I would have put him off the scent if Jimmu hadn't—"

"Perhaps you'd like to tell me exactly why your head needed clearing," Goro broke in.

Ryu shuffled his feet in embarrassment. "It's a private matter," he mumbled.

"You're part of a ninja team, Yasuda Ryu!" Goro said sharply. "There are no private matters. Tell me!"

Ryu spoke in a hoarse whisper. "It's Ichiro and Yuki," he said. "Whenever I see them together, it reminds me of what my life might have been. Today it was too much for me. I had to get away from camp for a while."

Goro nodded. "That sounds plausible," he said. He raised his voice. "Yuki, come and dress Jimmu's wound. The rest of you, start breaking camp. We leave for Tokoro Castle immediately."

A little later, as they were helping to load the wagon, Jimmu and Ren passed each other. Ren caught Jimmu's eye, and smiled. Jimmu blushed, and looked away; his feelings for Ren were like a betrayal of Takeko's memory.

Chapter 16
17TH – 20TH DAY, 5TH MONTH, 1575

For three days they travelled southwards towards Shima Province, where Tokoro Castle lay. Ichiro and Ren took the lead; Yuki drove the wagon, with Goro seated beside her; Jimmu and Ryu brought up the rear.

On the morning of the second day, Ryu had risen well before everyone else, so that he could shave his face and head in private. Afterwards it was difficult for him to adjust to his new appearance, and he kept rubbing his chin, and waving insects away from his bare scalp.

"You know what I can't get used to, Jimmu?" he joked. "Feeling flies landing on the top of my head!"

Jimmu did not reply. He was struggling with himself. The more he tried to prepare himself for what was to come, the more he was distracted by thoughts of Ren. He could not stop thinking about her, and it made him feel guilty.

You're a disgrace, he told himself. What about Takeko? What about the promise you gave to Yuki? You spend a year in a monastery, with no female company, and as soon as you leave, you make a fool of yourself over the first pretty face you meet. Where's your self-control?

But part of Jimmu knew that it was already too late for self-control. Ren was more than simply a pretty girl: she had touched something inside him, and reminded him of how powerful and unruly feelings could be.

Ryu leaned across his horse and slapped Jimmu's left arm. "Wake up, Jimmu!" he urged. "We can't have you falling out of your saddle."

"I wasn't asleep," said Jimmu. "I was thinking."

"You shouldn't!" Ryu warned. "Thinking too much leads to imagining, and imagining leads to fear. A samurai doesn't think – he reacts."

Jimmu did not agree. In his experience, whenever he reacted without thinking, it caused him problems.

*

At sunset on the third day, Goro called a halt in the coastal village of Nadamura. A group of villagers gathered to stare at the strangers. The village headman, Tajo, introduced himself to Goro.

"I'm delighted to meet you, Tajo!" Goro declared. "This evening, my friends and I will perform a puppet show in the village. Everyone is welcome to attend."

Tajo bowed his head in shame. "Nadamura is a poor village, Your Honour," he said. "We can't afford to pay for luxuries like puppet shows."

Goro sniffed the air. "Do I smell fish?" he asked.

"Yes, Your Honour," said Tajo. "It's mostly fishermen and their families who live here."

"Then why not pay us with fresh fish?" Goro suggested. He raised his voice. "The show will begin at nightfall!" he said. "The story will be the famous tale of Princess Kayuga and the Five Foolish Suitors. Tell all your friends!"

As they were tethering their horses, Ren spoke to Jimmu. "Are you nervous about performing in front of an audience?" she asked.

"Why should I be nervous?" Jimmu snapped.

"Don't you think I'm ready? Haven't you taught me well enough?"

Ren was puzzled by Jimmu's sudden hostility. "I'm only asking because I remember how nervous I was the first time," she said. "The trick is to understand that the audience's attention will be on the puppets, not you."

"I don't need any tricks," said Jimmu. "I've been in battle. A puppet show is nothing compared to that."

Ren's eyes showed her dismay. "Why are you being like this, Jimmu?" she said. "What happened to the you who smiles?"

"There isn't time to stand around and chat," said Jimmu. "We should be getting ready."

He turned his back on Ren, and walked towards the wagon. His emotions were as tangled as a clump of brambles: he wanted to push Ren away, but at the same time he wanted to draw her nearer.

Jimmu tried to picture Takeko in his mind, but she kept turning into Ren.

*

The stage was simple. Ichiro and Ryu draped a black sheet over one side of the wagon, and placed a low platform in front of it. Two torches lit the platform. Jimmu, Ren and Yuki dressed in black clothes, with hoods over their heads, and scarves covering their faces from the eyes down.

An audience of forty or more people had assembled, and they chattered loudly. Young children squirmed to free themselves from their mothers' arms, or ran about, shouting to one another.

Ichiro began to play a slow tune on his flute, and instantly the audience was still and silent.

Goro spoke into the silence. "Long, long ago, in a faraway province, an old basket weaver and his wife went into the forest to cut bamboo..."

From then on, Jimmu became lost in his performance.

The audience was lost too. They sighed at the beauty of the princess, and laughed at the antics of the suitors. At the end of the story, they let out an appreciative, "A-a-a-h!"

The villagers returned to their homes. The puppeteers packed away their equipment, and moved onto the nearby beach to make camp. Jimmu was still charged with the excitement of the performance, and strolled down to the tideline to calm himself. It was a clear night, and the rhythmic breaking of the waves on the shore was soothing.

Jimmu heard someone approaching, and knew that it was Ren, even before she spoke. "Goro sent me to tell you the food is ready," she said.

"I'm not hungry," said Jimmu.

Ren sighed. "What's wrong, Jimmu? You've been avoiding me since we left the camp in the forest."

Jimmu sensed that it was time for the truth. "Just after we met, I promised Yuki that I'd be no more than a friend to you, but I'm finding the promise difficult to keep," he said.

Ren looked down at the sand to avoid Jimmu's eyes. "I made Yuki the same promise, and I find it difficult too," she said. "What are we going to do?"

"Nothing," said Jimmu. "I must do what a samurai is meant to do, and ignore my personal feelings so that I can concentrate on saving Lady Takeko."

"It's different for me," Ren said. "I can't use the Samurai Code as an excuse for not doing something.

I'm a ninja. I enjoy the moment because the moment is all we have."

"Is that what you think I'm doing, making excuses?" said Jimmu.

Ren lifted her face. "Aren't you?" she said. "What's really holding you back, Jimmu, your samurai honour, or Lady Takeko?"

The question cut through to the centre of Jimmu's confusion. "If I knew the answer to that, I'd know what to do, but I don't," he said. "We shouldn't talk about this now, Ren, there are too many other things to think about. Let's complete our mission, and then we can talk again."

"When the mission's over, you'll take Lady Takeko back to her father, and I won't matter to you any longer," Ren said. "You'll probably brag to the other samurai about how you turned the head of a ninja girl!"

"You know I won't do that, and you'll always matter to me," said Jimmu.

Ren laughed in disbelief. "I met you for the first time eleven days ago, and I feel as if I've known you all my life," Ren said. "Why is that?"

It was another question that Jimmu could not answer.

Takeko watched without interest as the maid who had kept watch over her for the past ten days rolled out a sleeping bag on the floor of the honoured guests' room. Apart from introducing herself as Sora, the maid had said nothing to Takeko, but now she broke her silence.

"May I speak openly, My Lady?" she said.

"If you wish," replied Takeko with a sigh.

"I don't approve of how Lord Sabura has treated you," declared Sora. "It brings shame on him, and his clan. His father would never have done such a thing. I'm ashamed too, because I can't bring myself to tell Lord Sabura what a coward I think he is. If I can ease the misery of your captivity in any way, you only have to ask."

Takeko snorted. "Is this another of Lord Sabura's tricks?" she said. "Did he tell you to win my trust so that you can betray me, as Aki did? Does he take me for a fool?"

"I'm not like Aki, My Lady," said Sora. "Her kind is easily bought."

"If you want to help me ease my misery, fetch me a knife, or a cord so that I can hang myself!" Takeko said.

Sora bowed again. "I'm sorry, My Lady, but that's not possible," she said. "If any harm comes to you while you're in my care, Lord Sabura will have me put to death."

"Are you afraid of death, Sora?" asked Takeko.

"I'm not afraid of death, but I'm afraid of dying, My Lady," Sora replied.

"It's living that frightens me," said Takeko. "Death would be a relief."

Chapter 17

In the morning, the puppeteer troupe entered Shima Province. Ryu, who had added to his disguise by wrapping a black bandana around the lower half of his face, led the wagon along a high road that followed the coast. There was a fishing village in almost every bay they passed, and the ocean was dotted with boats sailing between rocky islands.

Over the next few days, the troupe made frequent stops, and put on many shows, slowly building up a reputation. Word about them spread quickly, and when they arrived at some villages, they found that they were expected, and an audience was already waiting for them.

The situation with Ren did nothing to calm Jimmu. Though he longed to be alone with her, when they were not working puppets together, Jimmu stayed out of

Ren's way, and they hardly spoke. However, he could not keep himself from thinking about her, especially before he fell asleep at night.

Jimmu was aware that his feelings for Takeko would never come to anything. She was a noblewoman: when the time came for her to marry — if they could rescue her from the dire situation she was in now — Lord Ankan would consult with the elders of the Choju Clan, and choose Takeko a husband who was her equal in rank. Jimmu was so inferior to her, that even a casual friendship between them would be regarded as highly improper.

It was different with Ren; she and Jimmu were both warriors. True, she had chosen the freedom of being a ninja, while he had dedicated himself to the service of Lord Ankan, but if they were serious about each other, perhaps they could make compromises.

Jimmu thought long and hard about what those compromises might be.

At noon on their third day in Shima, the puppeteers played in the little village of Josai, close to Tokoro

Castle. The audience was made up of villagers and their children, and a young man who stood out from the rest. He was well groomed and finely dressed, and he sat apart from the others to distance himself from them. At the end of the show, the young man walked over to Goro, and gave him a curt bow.

Jimmu, who was nearby, helping Yuki to pack away the puppets, listened closely to the conversation that followed.

"I am a personal attendant of Lord Hiki Sabura," the young man said. "Lord Sabura has heard favourable reports about the quality of your playing. He sent me to this village to judge whether your show might be suitable entertainment for His Lordship in Tokoro Castle this evening."

"We're honoured that Lord Sabura should take an interest in us!" said Goro. "What was your opinion of our humble efforts?"

The young man sniffed. "I was surprised by its delicacy," he said. "Many puppeteers resort to vulgarity and low humour to amuse the common people, but I saw nothing that would offend a person of refinement, such as His Lordship. Call at the castle gate before the drawbridge is raised at sunset. You will have to pass the night in the courtyard, but Lord Sabura will make sure that you are fed and made comfortable."

"Is His Lordship a generous man?" asked Goro.

"If you please him, he will give you a more than ample reward," said the young man. "Remember, before sunset. If you are late, you will incur His Lordship's displeasure." He made as if to go, then stopped, frowning. "Why does that fellow of yours keep his face covered?"

Goro drew on his storytelling skills. "He was once attacked by a jealous husband, who cut off his nose with a knife," he said. "He covers his face so that children won't be frightened of him."

"Make sure he keeps the scarf on when he is in Lord Sabura's presence," said the young man. He frowned at Ryu. "There is something oddly familiar about him," he said. "Is he from these parts?"

Jimmu tensed; if the young man recognized Ryu as Lord Sabura's disgraced samurai, the mission would be finished.

Goro chuckled. "He's from the far north of Mutsu

Province," he said. "Ask him yourself if you like, but his accent's so thick, I doubt if you'll understand a word he says!"

For a horrified second, Jimmu feared that the young man was about to question Ryu, but he simply bowed and took his leave.

When the young man had gone, Jimmu heaved a sigh of relief. "That was close, Goro!" he said. "I thought that he was on to us."

Goro shrugged. "We were safe enough," he said. "I've met his sort before – so conceited that he pays little attention to anyone but himself. Let's hope his master is just as vain."

Just outside Josai, the road ran into a dense forest of cedars. Ryu led the way off the main road onto a track that had been made by lumberjacks: clearings at the side of the track showed where they had been at work. The puppeteers stopped in one of the clearings, and made preparations for the task ahead of them.

Behind the cover of a clump of bracken, Jimmu undressed, and wound a length of rope around his waist before putting on the black breeches, jerkin and hood that Yuki had sewn for him. He rejoined the others, and watched as Ichiro and Yuki assembled a handcart from sections of wood slung under the wagon. When the handcart was complete, Ryu and Ichiro loaded the chest of puppets onto it, and a second chest.

"What's in there?" asked Jimmu.

"Spare costumes, heads and arms for the puppets, and a set of carpenter's tools, but they're in a shallow drawer that lifts out," Ichiro said. "We'll put the grappling hooks and our weapons in the space underneath."

"I hate not wearing my sword!" grumbled Jimmu. "I feel as though a part of me is missing."

"The guards at Tokoro won't let us near Lord Sabura if we're armed," Ryu pointed out.

"And besides, from now on we're no longer ninja or samurai," added Goro. "We're poor puppeteers who wish to perform for a rich nobleman. Be humble, and show respect! Don't forget to limp, Ryu, and Jimmu, don't stand so straight. Stoop a little, you're an entertainer, not a warrior."

Ren passed by, and she and Jimmu exchanged a quick smile.

Tomorrow, we'll talk, Jimmu promised himself. We'll discuss our differences, and find ways round them.

But for now, he pushed the thought to the back of his mind, and concentrated all his attention on the mission to rescue Takeko.

Lord Sabura stood smiling in the doorway of the honoured guests' room. He wore a dark red kimono, with a geometric pattern of lines and triangles woven in white.

Takeko was sitting on her sleeping mat; Sora was crouched on the floor, with her forehead pressed against the boards.

Lord Sabura's smile shrank. "Still in your shift, Takeko?" he said.

"Why should I bother getting dressed?" said Takeko.

"To please me, or anyone else who cares to look at you," Lord Sabura said. "If you do not make the most of your beauty, it will fade and go to waste. Chief maid, get out Lady Takeko's white silk kimono, and help her to wash and brush her hair. She must prepare for a special occasion."

"What special occasion?" said Takeko.

"A troupe of travelling players is going to put on a puppet show for us," Lord Sabura said. "I love puppet shows!"

"Is that why you try to turn people into puppets — so you can play with them?" said Takeko.

Lord Sabura beamed at her. "Sometimes your powers of perception astonish me, Takeko," he said. "I want you to look your best, for I can promise you that this evening will be a memorable one!"

Chapter 18

24TH DAY, 5TH MONTH, 1575

The puppeteers left the forest, and took the road that led to the main gate of Tokoro Castle. Ichiro walked in front, playing a lively tune on the flute. Behind him came Goro and Yuki – Yuki with her hand on Goro's shoulder to guide him. Next were Jimmu and Ren, holding up the puppets of the prince and princess. Ryu brought up the rear with the handcart, limping along with his head down.

As he approached the castle, Jimmu looked at it from a samurai's point of view. Though it was smaller than Mitsukage, Tokoro seemed more imposing. The walls and roofs were black, and it stood on a rocky outcrop that raised it above the surrounding countryside. A stream had been diverted to fill the moat around the castle, and to provide its inmates with a supply of water in case of a siege. Once the drawbridge at the end of the stone causeway was raised, the only way for enemy soldiers to gain entry was to swim the moat, and scale the outer wall.

Ren saw Tokoro differently. "It looks like a fat crow!" she murmured. "Crows are supposed to bring bad luck, aren't they?"

"Unless they visit Shinto temples," said Jimmu. "The priests there say that crows are messengers from the gods."

"Stop that whispering, you two!" Goro scolded. "Keep your minds on your puppets!"

The two guards on duty at the gate held nagatina – poles topped with curved blades as long as swords – which they crossed to bar the way as the puppeteers drew near. "What's your business here?" one of them demanded.

Goro bowed. "We've come to entertain His Lordship," he said.

"Kaito!" the guard barked.

A young soldier appeared.

"Go and ask the chief steward to come down here!" the guard ordered.

The soldier hurried away, and returned a few

minutes later in the company of a chubby man who had a superior manner. "I am Lord Sabura's chief steward," the man announced grandly. "Which of you is the leader?"

"I am, Your Honour," said Goro, bowing low.

"I've been told that your performance this afternoon was outstanding," the chief steward said.

"We try our best, Your Honour," said Goro. "If Lord Sabura's taste is for a simple tale told well, he will approve of our little show."

The chief steward was pleased by Goro's apparent humility. "Very well," he grunted to the guards. "Let them in!"

The chief steward led the puppeteers to a corner of the courtyard near the bathhouse. "You can wait here until Lord Sabura sends for you," he said. "You will be performing in the reception hall. Perhaps one of you would care to inspect it?"

"Go with His Honour, Ichiro," said Goro.

Ichiro followed the chief steward across the courtyard, and passed into the keep through a doorway.

Jimmu helped Ryu to unload the chest from the cart. Yuki and Ren opened the chest, and pretended to check the puppets.

Jimmu watched a detail of guards arrive to raise the drawbridge, and relieve the men at the gate. "They're all so young!" he commented to Ryu.

"Lord Hiki Yoshinori suffered heavy losses at the siege of Nagashino last year," said Ryu. "Most of the replacements haven't seen action yet."

Ichiro returned from his inspection of the reception hall, just as the shadows began to blur into dusk. "It's a good playing space," he said. "The screen doors have been shut, and the floor mats are clean. Servants are lighting the lamps, so I guess that we won't have to wait much longer."

A servant summoned the puppeteers to the reception hall, where the chief steward watched their every move as they prepared for the performance. Jimmu, Ren, Yuki and Ryu kept their features covered, Goro and Ichiro were barefaced. Ryu laid out the puppets in the order that they would be needed, and then the puppeteers took up their positions in front of a dais at one end of the room. Jimmu, Ren and Yuki faced the centre of the dais, with Goro and Ichiro to their right. Ryu stood behind, so he could hand the puppets to their operators.

When everything was ready, the chief steward made an announcement. "Lord Sabura will join us shortly," he said. "You will pay him homage by abasing yourselves. Do not speak to him directly unless he invites you to, and do not stare at him."

Four samurai entered the hall. Two mounted the dais, the other two went to stand beside the screen doors that opened out onto the garden. Unlike the guards that Jimmu had seen in the courtyard, the samurai were veterans, and swaggered as they walked. They stood to attention, with their arms folded across their chests.

"All bow in the presence of His Lordship!" cried the chief steward.

Jimmu crouched down, and pressed his forehead against the floor. He heard the tread of feet, and the rustling of silk robes.

"Lord Sabura grants his permission for the puppet

show to begin!" said the chief steward.

As Jimmu rose to his feet, he glanced quickly at the people seated on the dais, and was surprised to see a young woman and her maid among them. The young woman wore a white kimono. Her face had been powdered white, and her eyebrows and lips were black, after the fashion of the women at the Imperial Court in Kyoto. She looked like a beautiful statue carved from snow.

Jimmu's surprise turned to shock as he realized that it was Takeko. The girl he knew had gone. She was now a noblewoman, as remote and untouchable as the peak of a mountain. The closeness they had once shared vanished into the past; Jimmu saw more clearly now than ever that he could never be her equal in the way that he could with Ren. Jimmu felt as if he were saying goodbye to his old dreams about Takeko.

Ichiro took up his flute, and played a tune that Jimmu had not heard before, a slow melody, filled with plaintive dips and piercing trills. Goro started the story, and Jimmu worked the puppet of the woodcutter, moving it haltingly to show that the character was an old man who suffered from rheumatism. Jimmu forgot about Takeko, Lord Sabura, and the samurai, and entered the world of the tale.

The performance ended; the puppeteers bowed.

Lord Sabura saluted them with a wave of his fan. "Splendid!" he said. "I admire your skill, storyteller!"

"Your Lordship is too generous," replied Goro.

Lord Sabura smiled. "There is no need to be modest," he said. "I recognize your talent because I am something of a storyteller myself, and you have helped me to compose one of my best. Uncover your face, Yasuda Ryu, the time for pretence is over!"

Ryu pulled down his bandana. "I kept my word, My Lord," he said.

Jimmu frowned. "What word?" he exclaimed. "What are you talking about, Ryu?"

The two samurai on his left answered him by sliding back the screen doors to reveal twenty guardsmen, all holding drawn bows.

Too late, Jimmu saw that Ichiro had been right; Ryu had betrayed the puppeteers, and led them into a trap – but why?

"Take off your masks, all of you!" Lord Sabura exclaimed. "Let Lady Takeko see you!"

Jimmu slowly removed his bandana.

Takeko gazed at him in bewilderment for a few seconds, and then recognition finally showed in her eyes. "Jimmu!" she gasped.

"Yes – Jimmu," said Lord Sabura. "I promised Yasuda Ryu that I would take him back into my service if he could manage to find Jimmu, and trick him into coming to Tokoro."

Ryu looked down at the floor, and said nothing.

"What do you want with Jimmu, Sabura?" said Takeko.

"I want to see the expression on your face when you watch him die tomorrow morning, My Lady," Lord Sabura said. "Afterwards, I'll send his head to your father. Perhaps it will encourage him to change his mind about reinforcing Lord Nobunaga." He turned to the guards. "Tie the prisoners up, and take them away!" he commanded.

The puppeteers' hands were tied behind them. They were herded out of the keep and across the courtyard to the dungeon, which was set in the castle wall, not far from the drawbridge.

Jimmu was forced into a bare, narrow cell that had no window, and no light. He wriggled around until his back was resting against the wall, and tried to loosen the cord around his wrists, but it had been fastened too tightly, and eventually he gave up.

Memories came out of the dark to torment him, and his mind went back to his first meeting with Ryu at The Fortunate Swallows inn. Ryu must have followed him there from Mitsukage, and deliberately picked a quarrel with the bandits, knowing that Jimmu would come to the aid of a fellow samurai. And what had Ryu really told the Hiki scout before the attack on the ninja camp?

How easily Ryu had taken Jimmu in with his jokes and poems. He must have laughed inside at Jimmu's naivety. Jimmu was angry with himself; his eagerness to save Takeko had made him blind to Ryu's deceptions.

Still Jimmu could not quite believe that the companionship he had shared with Ryu was all a sham. After the fight on the Kyoto Road, Jimmu had felt a bond between them. Perhaps Ryu had felt the same, and been ashamed by what he was doing. That would explain Ryu's brooding silences as they travelled north.

The night before they reached Izumison, Ryu had said, "Sometimes, after you decide to do something for what you *think* is a good reason, it turns out that—" He had left the sentence unfinished. Had he been on the point of confessing the truth to Jimmu?

Jimmu groaned. Truth and lies, shame and betrayal did not matter any more. His dreams of freeing Takeko and serving Lord Ankan as a samurai had been shattered. To calm himself, Jimmu meditated on a riddle that Naoki had taught him in the monastery at Okamori.

Two men set out on a journey — which man is the older?

The riddle was meaningless and had no solution, but thinking of possible answers cleared Jimmu's mind of everything else, allowing him to focus on his final ordeal.

In the morning he would be put to death, and he was determined to die bravely.

Jimmu was not aware that he had fallen asleep until a sound woke him. He blinked at the darkness, his ears straining. He heard a scuffle outside the cell, followed by a stifled moan, and then a rasp as the beam that secured the door was drawn back.

The door swung open. Light from the torches in the corridor flooded the cell, dazzling Jimmu's eyes for a moment, and in that moment someone entered, and placed something on the floor at his feet. When Jimmu's eyes adjusted to the light, he saw that it was his sword; Ryu was kneeling beside it.

"What are you doing here?" demanded Jimmu.

"Keep your voice down!" Ryu hissed. "I'm going to

cut you loose, but first I want you to listen to me. I brought you and the others to Lord Sabura because I wanted to be reinstated as a samurai and because I wanted to be revenged on Ichiro. I did what Lord Sabura asked of me, but it cost me my self-respect. Being with you reminded me of the person I once tried to be, and made me see how far I'd fallen short. I can't let them execute you like a criminal, you deserve better than that. Take your sword and get out of here. If you're lucky, you can climb over the wall, swim the moat, and go back to the wagon for your horse. If you're not lucky—" Ryu shrugged. "At least you'll die fighting."

"Is this another trap, Ryu?" said Jimmu.

"You have to trust me," Ryu said. He leaned over, and cut Jimmu's bonds.

Jimmu rubbed his chafed wrists.

"Hurry up!" said Ryu. "I killed the guards in the corridor, but it won't be long before someone finds them, and sounds the alarm."

Jimmu picked up his sword. It felt good to have its familiar weight in his hands again. "I'm not going anywhere without Lady Takeko and the others," he said.

Ryu sighed.

"Trapped in a corner,
The field mouse shows the tomcat
What it means to fight," he muttered. "All right, Jimmu. We'll do it your way. Let's go and die in good company."

It did not take long for Jimmu and Ryu to free Goro, Ren, Ichiro and Yuki from their neighbouring cells. Afterwards, Ryu kept watch at the end of the corridor while the rest huddled together, talking in whispers.

"We must decide whether to carry on with our mission, or abandon it, and try to escape," said Goro.

"Why abandon it?" said Jimmu. "Our enemies are at a disadvantage. They think we're safely locked up. Our attack will be all the more unexpected."

"But can we rely on Ryu?" said Ichiro. "He's already betrayed us once. I'm surprised you didn't kill him as soon as you got your sword, Jimmu. I think I would have in your place."

"Jimmu showed wisdom, as well as restraint, Ichiro," Goro said. "Like it or not, we need Ryu.

When a man on the edge of a cliff loses his balance, he'll grab at a thorn bush to keep himself from falling." He sniffed. "I smell blood."

"Ryu killed the soldiers who were on guard," explained Jimmu.

"How many?" Goro said.

"Two," replied Jimmu.

"Excellent!" Goro said. "Put their bodies into a cell, and bar all the doors, so that nothing looks out of place. Ichiro and Yuki, strip the soldiers of their armour, and disguise yourselves as guards. Go outside and fetch in the handcart."

The team carried out Goro's instructions. The corpses of the guards were dragged into a cell. Ichiro and Yuki, dressed in armour, went out into the courtyard, and wheeled the handcart into the dungeon. They opened the false compartments, and distributed the equipment.

As he was slipping two throwing stars inside his jerkin, Jimmu noticed four strange objects at the bottom of the chest: four hand-sized earthenware balls with cloth fuses protruding from their tops.

"What are they?" Jimmu asked Ichiro.

"Chinese bombs," said Ichiro. "When they explode, they burst into splinters that fly around like musket bullets. Yuki and I will use them to create a diversion in the guardhouse."

"I didn't know there were such things," said Jimmu. "Why didn't you show them to me before?"

Ichiro grinned. "I'm a ninja," he said. "There are some secrets I like to keep to myself."

Ryu was winding a climbing rope around his waist. "At the far end of this corridor is a flight of steps that leads up onto the battlements," he said. "There'll be two guards on duty. Ichiro and Yuki can dispose of them, and take their place as the rest of us cross the courtyard to the door near the stable."

"Who made you our leader, Ryu?" snapped Ichiro.

"It was just a suggestion," Ryu said.

"And a good one," said Goro. "For tonight, forget your differences with Ryu, Ichiro. If you want to argue with him, save it until the morning."

Ren stepped over to Jimmu, grasped his hand and gave it a quick squeeze. "All the time I was in my cell, I couldn't think of anything but you," she whispered.

"No more talking!" said Goro. "From now on,

we're shadows in the dark. When we reach Lord Sabura's private apartments, Jimmu will go alone into Lady Takeko's room, and show his face so that she won't be alarmed. When he gives the signal, Ryu, Ren and I will go into the room, and climb out through the shutters. Does anyone wish to say anything?"

There was silence.

"Then let's go to work!" Goro said.

Chapter 20
24TH DAY, 5TH MONTH, 1575

Because the moat provided such an excellent defence, only a few guards were posted in Tokoro Castle at night, and they all faced outwards, not anticipating an attack from within. There was no moon; the only light came from torches in the courtyard, and Jimmu, Ryu, Ren and Goro kept in the shadows as they edged their way towards the stables.

Jimmu was not nervous, or excited. He relied on his senses to warn him of any danger, and the speed of his reflexes to deal with that danger if it threatened.

The team crept around the side of the stables, and gathered around the door that led into the keep. Goro slid a thin strip of metal between the door and the frame, and worked it upwards until it raised the latch. The door opened noiselessly, and the team went inside.

They were in a narrow corridor, lit by lanterns fixed to brackets on the walls. Jimmu and Ryu went ahead of Goro and Ren, with Ryu leading because he knew the way. Stepping cautiously, to avoid making the floorboards creak, they advanced to the end of the corridor, where it joined a second corridor that ran from left to right. Ryu glanced stealthily round the corner. He raised his hand, and clenched his fingers twice, to indicate the presence of two guards.

Moving with the elegant precision of dancers, Jimmu and Ryu stepped out from their cover.

The guards were positioned at the foot of a staircase. They had been on duty for hours, and were both drowsy. When two black-clad figures appeared in front of them, the guards were astonished. Before they had a chance to recover their wits, they were brought down by throwing stars. One man fell backwards; the other lay crumpled on the bottom stair.

The ninja team mounted the staircase, and this time it was Jimmu who reconnoitred.

The corridor that served Lord Sabura's private apartments was wider than the corridor on the ground floor, and its ceiling was higher. The four veteran samurai who had been at the puppet show were standing guard in front of two doorways; a pair of guardsmen armed with nagatina had taken up position at the far end of the corridor.

Jimmu hand-signalled the others.

Goro and Ren sprang from the head of the stairs to the centre of the corridor, and launched throwing stars at the nearest pair of samurai. Goro's star found its target, and the samurai collapsed, clutching at his throat. Ren's star narrowly missed, as the samurai managed to duck at the last instant.

Goro and Ren moved aside, and let Jimmu and Ryu take their places. Jimmu had drawn his sword; Ryu was armed with a sickle and chain.

The samurai Ren had missed bore down on Ryu, holding his sword at an angle that showed he was intending to use a diagonal stroke. Ryu crouched, swung the chain so that it wrapped itself around the samurai's ankles, and pulled the man off balance. The samurai crashed down, and Ryu sank the point of the sickle into his chest.

The two remaining samurai closed in on Jimmu. He stood with his body turned sideways to them, his sword raised so that the back of the blade almost touched his cheek.

Once again, time ran slowly for Jimmu, and his senses were at a pitch where he was aware of everything. The body language of the samurai told him that they were about to strike simultaneously, and he knew exactly where each blow would land.

Steel glinted in the lamplight as Jimmu parried, wheeled, feinted and slashed. The cutting edge of his sword sliced open the jugular vein of the first samurai, and severed the sword arm of the second samurai at the elbow. Jimmu ended the man's agony with a quick thrust to the heart, and then turned to face the guardsmen, who were advancing on him with their nagatina lowered.

The guards were not as sure of themselves as the samurai had been, and they both gave off the sour smell of fear.

Jimmu detected the smell, and hoped that the guards' fear would give him an advantage. He was in a perilous situation: the nagatina was a formidable weapon, the length of its shaft keeping the bearer safely beyond the reach of any swordsman.

The guard to Jimmu's right jabbed at him, aiming for his midriff. Jimmu jumped high, tucking his legs beneath him, then straightened his left leg in a vicious kick that he had been taught by Yuki. His heel caught the guard's chin, forcing the man's head back so violently that his neck snapped with a sharp crack.

Jimmu misjudged his landing, and sprawled across the floor. He was certain that he was about to die: it would be impossible for him to get to his feet before the second guard struck.

But the guard was inexperienced; he had never used his nagatina on an actual person, only a dummy stuffed with straw. Instead of running Jimmu through, he hesitated. In that moment of hesitation, Goro's throwing star hit him between the eyes. The guard's knees buckled, and he collapsed.

Jimmu looked round.

Ryu pointed to a doorway, and his mouth mimed, "Ta-ke-ko."

Jimmu went to the door, and opened it just wide enough for him to slip inside.

The room was in darkness.

"Takeko?" whispered Jimmu. "Don't be afraid, it's me – Jimmu!"

It was several seconds before Jimmu was able to see clearly enough to make out details. He saw a low table, a set of shelves, a wardrobe, and a bed rolled out across the middle of the floor.

The bed was empty; Takeko was not in the room.

Jimmu's shoulders sagged in disappointment.

What's gone wrong? he asked himself. Has Takeko been moved somewhere else? Did Ryu make a mistake?

Mystified, Jimmu returned to the corridor – and entered a scene from a nightmare.

Goro, Ryu and Ren were as still as actors frozen in a tableau. Behind them, the blood of the slain samurai was still running down the walls. They were all staring at Lord Sabura's bedchamber.

Lord Sabura stood in the doorway, holding a dagger to Takeko's neck. "Stay back!" he ordered Jimmu. "Come any closer and I'll kill her!"

Ryu spoke in a quiet voice. "Has it come to this, My Lord, hiding behind a woman?" he said.

"You are a great disappointment to me, Yasuda Ryu!" retorted Lord Sabura.

Just then, the Chinese bombs planted by Ichiro and Yuki exploded, and four loud reports rang out.

Lord Sabura instinctively looked in the direction of the explosions, taking his eyes off the ninja.

Jimmu and Ryu acted as one. Ryu sprang on Lord Sabura, and wrenched the hand holding the dagger away from Takeko, while Jimmu pulled her to safety. Lord Sabura and Ryu tussled, stumbled, and fell together in the doorway. Though their fight lasted only a few seconds, to both men it felt like a lifetime. They rolled this way and that, gasping and grimacing, Ryu struggling to keep a firm hold of Lord Sabura's knife hand; Lord Sabura straining to break free. As Ryu twisted his body on top of his opponent, his right ear came close to Lord Sabura's mouth, and Lord Sabura sank his teeth into it. The unexpected pain caused Ryu to relax his grip. Lord Sabura stabbed him in the back, again and again.

Jimmu strode over to the doorway, and raised his sword.

Lord Sabura looked into Jimmu's eyes. "Spare me!" he whimpered. "I will give you anything you want. I will make you rich."

Jimmu lopped off his head with a sweeping blow.

Goro crouched, and pressed his fingers to the base of Ryu's left ear to feel for a pulse. "Yasuda Ryu is dead," he announced. "He has paid for his betrayal."

Jimmu gazed down at Ryu's corpse, and hoped that he had regained his self-respect before the end.

Attracted by the sounds of shouting, Ren unlatched one of the shutters in the corridor, and peered out. "The bombs have started a fire," she said. "The whole guardhouse is alight. They've formed a bucket-chain to try and put it out."

Goro stood upright, and unwound a rope and grappling hook from around his waist. "Then we should take our leave while the Hiki guards are otherwise occupied," he said. "Are you accustomed to climbing, My Lady?"

"Not dressed like this!" said Takeko.

"Here, let me help," Ren offered. She drew out a knife, and sheared the hem of Takeko's kimono to knee height.

"We'll go out through Lord Sabura's room, climb down, and then swim across the moat," said Goro.

Dismay showed in Takeko's face. "But I can't swim!" she protested.

"You won't have to," Jimmu reassured her. "Just keep hold of me, and I'll do the swimming for us both."

It was a difficult climb. Ren went first, negotiating projecting eaves and dragon finials to place ropes for the others. As he descended, Jimmu heard voices barking out urgent orders, the clatter of horses' hoofs, and the creaking crash of collapsing timbers. To the north, the sky was stained red with light from the fire, and a column of smoke rose above the castle. Jimmu shut out the sights and sounds, and concentrated on Takeko, holding her steady and whispering encouragement as they went.

At last, the team reached the sloping sides of the castle's stone foundations. They picked their way down the slope, and slipped into the moat: Goro first, followed by Jimmu and Takeko, and Ren.

It was hard going for Jimmu. His wet robes dragged at his limbs, and because he had to support Takeko, he could only use one arm to swim; but despite his weariness and discomfort, Jimmu was filled with a sense of triumph. He had succeeded, despite Lord Ankan's disapproval, and Ryu's treachery.

Light from the burning castle cast a murky glow over the moat, but Jimmu was not aware of it, until he noticed that he could make out Ren's face as she swam parallel with him.

And Jimmu was not the only one to notice the firelight illuminate the moat. When he and Takeko were just over halfway across, an arrow splashed into the water close to his face, followed by a second arrow that came even closer.

Ren began to thrash her arms and legs. "Hey!" she shouted. "Over here! Over here!"

"Ren?" said Jimmu, mystified.

"Go!" Ren told him.

Jimmu suddenly understood: Ren was making a noise to attract the attention of the bowmen who were firing on them, to give him and Takeko a better chance of escaping. "Hold your breath!" he warned Takeko, and then he held his own breath, and dived down below the surface.

Total darkness swallowed Jimmu and disorientated him. He kicked out, not knowing if he was going in the right direction, feeling his pulse pounding in his ears. Takeko dug him in the ribs with her elbow. Jimmu guessed she was signalling that she could not hold her breath any longer, and he risked bringing her up for air.

No arrows greeted their appearance above the water. The entire keep of Tokoro Castle was now ablaze, and any guards still on duty were probably too occupied with saving themselves to worry about escaping enemies.

Jimmu could see no sign of Ren.

Takeko was shivering, and her teeth chattered. "I'm cold, Jimmu!" she mumbled, and he knew he would have to swim on for her sake.

By the time he reached the far bank of the moat, Jimmu was exhausted, and grateful for Goro's help to pull Takeko out of the water.

"Is Ren with you?" Jimmu asked.

"No," said Goro. "I heard her shout a little while ago, and then someone cried out but I couldn't tell who it was."

Jimmu felt as if a heavy weight had been loaded inside his chest. "I'm going back to look for her," he said.

"A ninja never goes back!" Goro said sternly.

"I'm not a ninja," said Jimmu.

Jimmu did not have to search for long. After he had swum a dozen strokes, he saw a black shape in the water, and he knew that it was Ren. She was floating face down, with an arrow protruding from between her shoulder blades. Jimmu saw that there was nothing he could do, and swam back towards Goro and Takeko. His victory smelled of blood and smoke, and tasted of ashes.

Chapter 21

As he ran through the woods with Takeko and Goro, Jimmu was not aware of where he was going; his mind was too full of Ren.

When they arrived back at camp, there was no sign of Ichiro and Yuki.

Goro bowed to Takeko with elaborate formality. "Please forgive our rough and ready ways, My Lady. We are not used to receiving noblewomen," he said. "If you would care to enter the wagon, you can take off your wet things, and you'll find enough blankets to make up a bed of sorts. I regret that it will be necessary for you to keep inside the wagon until we are safely clear of Ise Province."

Takeko frowned. "Who are you exactly?" she asked.

"My name is Goro. Jimmu will explain everything to you later," he said.

Takeko was not satisfied by this reply, but she was worn out by the effort of her escape, and she climbed inside the wagon without further comment.

Goro turned to Jimmu. "Lady Takeko can rest, but we can't," he said. "We must harness up the animals, so we can leave as soon as Ichiro and Yuki get here."

"And what if they don't come back?" said Jimmu.

"Then we'll have to leave without them," said Goro.

A wave of misery almost overwhelmed Jimmu, and he directed it at Goro. "I don't understand you, Goro!" he snapped. "Ren is dead, but you act as if nothing happened. Don't you care?"

"I grieve for my fallen comrade in my own way," said Goro.

"But Ren was more than a comrade to me!" Jimmu exclaimed.

"Then it's partly yourself that you're grieving for," said Goro. "You have a decision to make, Jimmu. You can dwell on what might have been until it drives you out of your mind, or you can do what needs to be done to complete the mission, and return Lady Takeko to her father, which is what Ren would have done if you had been killed and she lived."

Jimmu knew that Goro was right: if the mission failed, Ren's death would be pointless; he owed it to her to carry on.

It was more than an hour before Ichiro and Yuki turned up, still dressed in the Hiki guards' uniforms. When Goro told them that Ren and Ryu were dead, Ichiro said nothing, but pain showed in his eyes; Yuki lowered her head to hide her tears.

The team spent the rest of the night travelling. At sunrise, they crossed the border of Ise Province, and carried on well into the morning, before finally halting on the outskirts of a village.

Jimmu fell asleep as soon as he lay on his sleeping mat, and no dreams came to trouble him.

It was long past noon when Yuki woke Jimmu. She gave him a bowl of cold rice and vegetables, and he sat to eat. Goro and Ichiro were chatting to each other near the wagon. Someone else was sitting a short distance away from them, and Jimmu's insides lurched because he thought it was Ren; then he realized that it was Takeko, dressed in the boy's clothes that Ren used to wear.

Goro motioned to Jimmu. "Come here!" he called. "We have business to discuss."

Jimmu got up reluctantly, and walked over to the wagon. Ichiro greeted him with a nod, and went to join Yuki, so that Goro and Jimmu could talk in private.

"So, Jimmu, the time has come for us to part," Goro began. "You must return Lady Takeko to Mitsukage Castle, while Yuki, Ichiro and I head for our village in Iga." Goro reached inside his jerkin, took out a folded paper, and gave it to Jimmu.

"What's this?" Jimmu said.

"It's a request for Lord Ankan to donate twenty gold pieces to the Shrine of the Sun Goddess at Uji-Tachi," explained Goro. "The gold will be an expression of His Lordship's gratitude for his daughter's safety. I'll collect the money from the abbot of the shrine when I next pass through Ise."

"You're not going to keep Lady Takeko until payment has been made?" said Jimmu.

Goro shrugged. "I would if I were dealing with another man, but Choju Ankan has great integrity. I trust him to do the honourable thing."

Jimmu slid the letter inside the sash at his waist.

"Will you listen to an old man's observation without taking offence?" Goro asked cautiously.

"Are you going to give me the benefit of your wisdom?" said Jimmu.

"I hope so," Goro said. "It seems to me that whenever you stray from the path of the warrior, you find unhappiness, Jimmu. Perhaps you should learn a lesson from that."

"You mean I should stay true to the Samurai Code?" said Jimmu.

"I mean that you should stay true to yourself," Goro said. "Remember who you are, Shimomura Jimmu, and don't fight against it. No good will come of trying to be someone else." Goro sniffed, and rubbed the back of his hand across his nose. "That's more than enough wisdom from me!" he declared. "Go and talk to Lady Takeko. She needs to know what's going on."

Jimmu became tense. "I've got nothing to say to her," he muttered.

"She's your lord's daughter, and she's your responsibility," Goro reminded him. "Go to her!"

Jimmu sat next to Takeko without looking at her. An awkward silence settled over them, until Takeko broke it at last. "Who are those people, Jimmu?" she said.

"Ninja," said Jimmu. "I asked them for help after Lord Ankan refused to attack Tokoro Castle."

"My father sent you to them?" Takeko said.

"I was tricked by Yasuda Ryu, Lord Sabura's samurai," said Jimmu. "He took me to the ninja, and led us into a trap, but then thought better of it and set us free."

Takeko sighed. "It's strange," she said. "I thought that when we saw each other again, we'd both be glad, but you're not glad, are you, Jimmu?"

"A friend of mine was killed last night," said Jimmu.

"Was that Ren?" Takeko said. "The woman mentioned something about her."

"Yuki!" snapped Jimmu. "The woman's name is Yuki."

He could not keep the bitterness out of his voice. Yuki had risked her life for Takeko, and Takeko had not even bothered to ask her name.

"I'm sorry Ren died, but it isn't my fault, Jimmu," Takeko said.

"I didn't say that it was, My Lady," said Jimmu.

Takeko plucked a blade of grass from the turf in front of her, and laced it between her fingers. "You used to call me Takeko when we were alone together," she said.

"That was a different time. We were younger," said Jimmu. "You shouldn't have allowed me the liberty, My Lady."

"That girl — Ren," said Takeko. "Was she a close friend?"

"She was special," said Jimmu. "Funny, courageous, graceful. I don't expect to meet anyone like her again. If I could—" He broke off, choking on his emotion.

Takeko rolled the blade of grass into a ball, and flicked it away. "We can't go back to the way things used to be, can we, Jimmu?" she said.

"No, My Lady," said Jimmu.

*

At sunset, Jimmu mounted Ryu's horse, and let Takeko ride the bay mare. There were no drawn-out goodbyes. Jimmu saluted Goro, Yuki and Ichiro with a brisk bow, and then turned his horse's head to the north-west, and drove his heels into its flanks to urge it into a trot. Takeko rode by his side; neither of them looked back.

Chapter 22

Jimmu and Takeko reached Mitsukage Castle early the following morning. The inhabitants were already busy making ready for war. Companies of soldiers drilled in the main courtyard. Smiths worked at their forges. Samurai carefully sharpened their swords on whetstones. Quartermasters filled sacks with rice from the storehouses. Armourers opened crates of new muskets, and distributed their contents. Local farmers brought in mules that were needed to make up pack trains.

Takeko went straight to her father's private apartments; Jimmu reported to Captain Hankei.

The captain was in his quarters, seated behind a small table. He was delighted when Jimmu announced the news of Takeko's safe return, but as he questioned Jimmu further, and learned more details of the attack on Tokoro Castle, Jimmu could sense the captain's mounting disapproval.

When Jimmu finished his account, he presented Captain Hankei with the piece of paper Goro had given to him.

"What's this?" the captain demanded.

"It's a message for Lord Ankan from the leader of the ninja," said Jimmu. "It contains a request for payment."

Captain Hankei struck the table with his fist. "The impudence of it!" he exclaimed. "You shouldn't have had dealings with those people, Jimmu. They're despicable!"

"I don't agree, Captain Hankei," said Jimmu. "I found much to admire in them. In their own way, ninja are as dedicated as samurai."

Captain Hankei's face turned red with indignation. "There can be no comparison between a class of noble warriors, and a gang of common criminals!" he snapped. "Contact with ninja has corrupted you, Jimmu. What became of the ideals you once cherished?"

"If I had followed my ideals, I would be dead, and

Lady Takeko would still be a prisoner," Jimmu pointed out. "I did what was necessary."

Captain Hankei was not happy with Jimmu's answer, but he made no comment on it. "I'll take the ninja's message to His Lordship at once," he muttered, "though I don't know what his reaction will be. Until ordered otherwise, you'll confine yourself to my quarters, Jimmu. Lord Ankan will deal with you in due course."

While Jimmu sat patiently waiting, Goro's advice about staying true to himself kept echoing through his mind. Was it true? Had he been pretending to be somebody else to avoid facing up to who he was? Ren had died trying to help him free Takeko, and he felt in her debt. Was becoming Lord Ankan's loyal samurai enough to repay her, or did she deserve more?

Something else that Goro had said came back to Jimmu, and he whispered it aloud. "Perhaps it's your destiny to restore your family's honour."

Shimomura Jimmu: was that the person he was struggling so hard not to be?

Captain Hankei came back into the room. He did not return Jimmu's bow. "Lord Ankan wishes to see you," he said.

"Is His Lordship angry with me?" asked Jimmu.

"Lord Ankan does not discuss his personal feelings with the captain of the guard," Captain Hankei said. "You must judge his mood for yourself."

Lord Ankan was sitting cross-legged on the rush matting that covered the floor of his apartment. Goro's note, and a scroll sealed with a blob of red wax, were laid out in front of him. His Lordship acknowledged Jimmu's bow. "Sit down, Jimmu," he said.

Lord Ankan looked careworn. The dark circles under his eyes had not gone away. "Once again, I have to thank you for saving my daughter's life, Jimmu," he said. "I have ordered gold to be sent to the shrine at Uji-Tachi. This note makes it appear that an enterprising band of ninja rescued Takeko because they saw a chance to turn an easy profit. I owe you a debt of gratitude. However—"

"Forgive my interruption, My Lord, but I must speak!" said Jimmu.

Lord Ankan nodded. "Go on."

"My Lord, I'm not worthy to enter your service," said Jimmu. "I acted against your wishes. I may have had good reason for doing so, but such disobedience cannot go unpunished."

Lord Ankan sighed. "Though it grieves me to admit it, you are right, Jimmu," he said. "The first duty of a samurai is to follow his lord's orders. You ignored mine. It is a pity. I had high hopes of you. All is not lost, however." Lord Ankan waved his hand over the documents in front of him. "This scroll is a letter from me, commending you to Lord Oda Nobunaga. Take it to him, and he will receive you into his service."

"This is better than I deserve, My Lord," Jimmu said.

Lord Ankan broke eye contact with Jimmu, and spoke in a low voice. "There is another reason why you must leave Mitsukage, Jimmu. It is obvious from the way Takeko talks that she still feels tenderness towards you. I cannot allow these feelings to continue. When you go, it will hurt her, but a little pain now is preferable to a greater pain in the future. You understand?"

"Yes, My Lord," said Jimmu.

Lord Ankan nodded. "Goodbye, Jimmu. I shall follow your progress with interest."

Jimmu stood up, and bowed low. "Goodbye, My Lord," he said.

He went from Lord Ankan's apartment to the stables, where he saddled up Ryu's horse, and rode out of the main gate of Mitsukage Castle.

For most of his life, Jimmu had felt tainted by his father's shame. Now he had a chance to cleanse himself, a chance to make his family name something to be proud of. He would have to work hard to gain Lord Oda Nobunaga's approval, but if he managed to prove himself, Lord Nobunaga could use his influence on the Emperor to bring about the restoration of the Shimomura Clan.

"Is that enough, Ren?" he murmured.

As he spoke, a pair of white herons sailed over his head, screeching to each other.

Jimmu took it as an answer.

Andrew Matthews has been writing for fun since he was seven, but was a teacher for twenty-three years before becoming a full-time author. He has written over sixty books for children and teenagers, including *Cat Song*, which was nominated for the Smarties Book Prize in 1994, and the critically acclaimed *Love Street*. He is a hugely versatile writer, and has retold many myths, legends and classic stories, as well as writing his own original novels.

Andrew lives in Reading with his wife and their cat.

Also by Andrew Matthews

THE
WAY
OF THE
WARRIOR

Truth and honour are the way of the warrior.

Jimmu is haunted by the death of his father, and his destiny is clear – he must train as a samurai, so that one day he will take revenge against his father's rival, and restore his family name.

But just as blood is about to be spilled, Jimmu discovers something that casts doubt on his life's mission. Now Jimmu must change his fate, before his own life is placed in jeopardy...

ISBN 9780746076354

"A real page-turner complete with a last-minute twist."
Flapjack

For more gripping adventures
log on to
WWW.FICTION.USBORNE.COM